T0194194

A Bridge of Wood

by

Nettye Sollars-Downhour

iUniverse, Inc.
Bloomington

A Bridge of Wood

This is a work of fiction. All of the characters, names, incidents, organizations, and dialogue in this novel are either the products of the author's imagination or are used fictitiously.

iUniverse books may be ordered through booksellers or by contacting:

iUniverse
1663 Liberty Drive
Bloomington, IN 47403

www.iuniverse.com

1-800-Authors (1-800-288-4677)

ISBN: 978-1-4502-7957-4 (SC)
ISBN: 978-1-4502-7958-1 (ebook)

Printed in the United States of America
iUniverse rev. date:2/14/11

Preface

In the beginning, when God made wood, when He made His first tree, I can just visualize the scene. Being accustomed to perfection as He was, God just had to pause there, smiling, taking a few seconds longer, all knowing and joyous over what He'd done. There before Him, in perfect glory, stood a tree. A tree that down through eons of life to come would breathe-in man's violations on Nature, digesting it, while exuding-out purity for man as succulence for existence as that man schlepped along, too often indifferently, living his life. A tree so multi-useful, yet perhaps quite ordinary amid His massive realm of creation.

It is a small piece from just such a tree, sturdy, lustrous and elegant, that will bridge across several generations of a family named Bennett. This spanning bridge, this piece of that tree, will serve as a tie between these generations…an unobtrusive tie, seemingly insignificant, yet affecting…enhancing…ever on-going.

Long ago in time, 'way back in 1850, or there about, it was from a forest of such trees that Ethan Bennett, a kind, hard-working, middle-aged man, carefully chose just the right tree. From this tree Ethan would shape a piece of wood into a project forming in his mind. A project that was to be a special gift…a kitchen worktable…for his wife, RoseMarie. A project that generations later, pieces from the wood of that same kitchen table, worn and broken, laying stored in a shed, yet still revered with historic sentiment, would become 3 lustrous candlesticks.

Unknowingly, Ethan Bennett would head-up a household among the first of this story's several generations. Also, unknowingly to Ethan, this very piece of wood was destined to be the bridge that would span these generations.

Truly, it was long ago, back there in 1850, or there about, when being quite knowledgeable concerning trees, Ethan was ready with his sharpened axe and crosscut saw. He'd been eyeing some tall oaks growing in a certain portion of his family's mighty forest. He knew the wood of a white oak would beautify as it aged.

Acknowledgements

I am indebted to my granddaughter, Johnna McCreary, a resident of Omaha, Nebraska, for her loving help in researching the current layout of that area's highways, streets, and housing developments.

To my son, Greg Hollen, a resident of Newburgh, Indiana, I give my heartfelt thanks and deep appreciation for his help in gathering historical material of that area. Through his efforts I gained authentic information concerning that city's beginning in the very early 1800s, and of its role during the Civil War.

To my proofreader, Daphne Marcotte, I thank for her time, patience, and verbal support.

To my daughter, Toni Allison, and my son, Ted Hollen, I am lovingly grateful for their background help and support.

With my own birth occurring 2 years before the end of WWI, and with my growing-up and living the bulk of my life in the mid-west, I could act as my own encyclopedia, along with conferring with my computer software, Encarta

Table of Contents

ONE

A Package at the Door

Driving at the speed of the Omaha evening traffic, Gail swung onto the left lane of I-80 East. Sitting-up straight in her seat, every ounce of her being was alert to the occasion. With the right-hand turn signal tick-tick, ticking, at each slightest opportunity she began nudging over. She had to get through those never ending streams of vehicles into the outer right hand lane. As usual, each driver was rushing, bent on getting to his own particular someplace.

To Gail, this getting over quickly into that farthest lane was a routine part of one more workday's evening accomplishments. And, as always, as was true with each of these evenings, she was making it just in time. Just a short way ahead, she could see the lane veering off south. It would become Kennedy Freeway and would take her into Omaha's abutting neighbor, Bellevue, and home.

Rounding that curve onto Kennedy, she let out a little, "whoo-sh," an audible sigh of relief. And she began to settle back a bit. Once more, that short but monstrous stretch of Interstate 80 East, that 5-evenings a week "tiger," was whipped. Once more, her "getting home from work" challenge had been faced and overcome!

Easing into a more relaxed mood, Gail allowed herself to smile. She loved her work, but being head of her department with a number of workers answering to her, the days could get pretty hectic.

Always, as the office clock was nearing quitting time, she was ready to oblige it, although she was meticulous in seeing that each paper on her desk had been handled in its proper business way. And she demanded the same from each of her workers. Thus her entire department appeared organized and neat, ready for the next business day.

Driving now, mentally, already she was beginning to step into the realm of her other job. Her other equally important job as wife and mother. But, by now, Gail, the innate organizer, had this role pretty much down pat. This job, too, had its little "tigers" to contend with, its little up-sets, but with Bruce and her as active co-CEOs pulling together, their little Hinton household was happy and on-going.

Exiting off the freeway onto Cornhusker Road, then a few more turns, and Gail was at the front area of the Logan Fontenelle Junior High School. A few moments of idling, jockeying, waiting patiently among the other parents to take her turn, she pulled in along curbside.

Already she'd spotted her son, Ethan, waiting, watching for her. He lost no time in throwing his backpack onto the passenger side floor, then giving his mom a grin of greeting, he jumped in.

Gail pulled out into traffic as Ethan fastened his seat belt, settling in beside her, and they were on their way. Not too far ahead was their Hidden Hills community and home.

Driving along, Gail glanced over at her young son. At the moment, he was scanning a bit of paper he'd taken from his pocket. Likely, it was something to do with a homework assignment. Ethan was 11 years old, and he more or less lived in his own little world.

She smiled, thinking *if only he could figure it out, he'd realize his little world is actually pretty benign. It seems his biggest concern right now is that he detests his name!*

In Gail's motherly knowing way she was thinking to herself, *he has so much growing up to do, so much developing yet to do!* Glancing at him, filling with a surge of pride, she thought, *gosh, but he is looking so much like his dad. He's heading toward being the handsome heartbreaker that Bruce was back when I first met him!*

With that, Gail's thoughts began running at random, going back to those days of the very first of her coming to Nebraska. Those days at Kearney, Nebraska, and her enrollment at Kearney College...

She'd been a young college freshman, coming as a stranger from her home in California. She'd been so excited. Also she'd been so scared and so lonely. But, almost from the first, there had been this guy, this good-looking guy with his warm smile. He was in one of Gail's classes. And this guy was Bruce Hinton. Nebraska was his home state, so he was already familiar with Kearney and the college. From the very first, his big dream was to become a certified public accountant.

Gail was smiling, remembering. Those four years of Kearney had ended with a flood of wonders. Wonders that involved degrees for the two seniors, a State Board certification fulfilling Bruce's dream, new Omaha jobs for the two of them, and exciting plans in the making for their soon-to-be marriage.

Turning now into Hidden Hills, with only a few blocks to their house, Gail thought, *my gosh, I can't believe it! It's been 19 years since I first came to Nebraska! Holly is already 14 years old! Am I getting old, or what!*

Approaching their house and seeing the still closed garage door, Gail knew that Holly had not beaten them home. It was the family's little custom that the first to arrive in the evening opened the garage door. Both kids knew the number combination to punch manually for this. Entering the garage, they could access the house through the pass-way door.

Holly was in 10th grade level at Bellevue High School, and this week it was the neighbor's turn to pick her up along with the neighbor's own daughter.

Bruce would be the last to arrive home from his day. As a rule, that would be 5 o'clock or so. By then, Gail, would have the family dinner about ready. Plus a load of laundry going in the washer.

Pressing her door opener remote as she was turning into the driveway, Gail pulled into her side of the garage. Gathering up his stuff, Ethan went on into the house.

Retrieving her purse along with her brief case, Gail walked out the wide-open doorway and across the walk to the front entryway of the house. She would get the mail on her way in.

There, setting by the front door, was a package. With her hands already full, and juggling a bit to get the door unlocked, Gail stooped down to better see the box, thinking, *gosh, I wonder what this can be…I'm not expecting anything.*

Setting her things inside the foyer, she went back out to get the package. Ethan was already in his own room, such triviality as the day's mail commonplace to him.

The package was a fairly big box, sent via UPS. It was addressed to Mr. & Mrs. Bruce Hinton, and it had been sent by Mrs. Mollie Hill, from Danville, Illinois.

"My gosh," Gail said aloud. "That's my grandfather's sister. My old great aunt, Mollie!" and she carried the box into the kitchen, anxious to get it open.

Packed so very carefully, inside the box, were 3 candlesticks. As she lifted them out, one by one, she set them on the countertop. Gail could see that they were old. One looked to be about 4 inches high, one about 6 inches high, and the third one was about 8 inches. They were made of wood, but there was such an unusual luster about them. Gail studied them, almost in reverence. She could see they were quite beautiful.

Also, in the box, was an envelope with a note from Gail's Aunt Mollie.

Although she was in a hurry, Gail took time to read the short letter. The note was neatly typed. It had been done on a typewriter or a computer. Gail's thoughts were, *hm-m, do you suppose she's into computers…she's just got to be so-o old! My grandfather's been dead for several years.*

The note read, "My dear niece, Gail, I've made the decision that you and your family should be the ones now to be entrusted with these old candlesticks. They are heirlooms made from wood dating back many generations ago. The wood, originally, was from a table made in 1850 by one of our ancestors, an Ethan Bennett. Your family tree will show that Ethan is a grandfather of yours with many 'greats' preceding that title. I have no doubts about your family's loving the candlesticks, and I am positive about your taking good care of them always. Contact me for more family information." In pretty handwriting, it was signed "Aunt Mollie." She had also included her phone number.

"Oh, my gosh!" Gail said aloud. As she gathered up the packing, taking it to the laundry room for later disposal, she was realizing that this gift was something very special.

Hurriedly, she changed into more comfortable casual clothes, then began setting out preparations for the family dinner.

Gail heard a rush of girl noises in the garage telling her that Holly was home and that she wasn't alone. With the opening of the pass through door, Holly announced to her mother, "I'm home, Mom, and Meredith's going to be with me 'til dinnertime! We'll be in my room if you need me…we've got some research to do for our project! Okay?" but before Gail could get in an answer, that little eddy of girl stuff had already whirled into Holly's room, and that door had closed behind them!

Gail just smiled. Girls! How she loved them.

Meredith was Holly's own age, and they'd been friends forever. It was her mom, the neighbor, whose turn this week it was to pick-up the kids from school.

Holly was always deep into some project. Bruce and Gail still had stars in their eyes from her recent one. What a to-do there'd been over that one. Imagine being parents of a child whose essay was judged #1 in a statewide contest!

Gail set out the wok on the kitchen island work center, plugging it into the built-in outlet. She'd already laid out the boneless chicken breast tenders on the cutting board. Pouring a bit of olive oil in the wok, she began dicing bite-size pieces of the meat. As she amassed a little pile, she gathered it up, dropping it into the wok, stirring it around. Tonight, dinner was scheduled to be "stir-fry."

As she worked, she kept noting the time. At a certain point, she would put on a pot of rice, setting the timer for 14 minutes once the water boiled.

As the chicken pieces were slowly sizzling, and with Gail stirring them around every so often, she began setting the dining area table. The time was nearing when she'd be hearing Bruce coming in.

By now, Ethan had joined her in the kitchen, sitting at the snack bar side of the work center. He had some school work laid out around him and was sipping from a can of soda. He liked getting his homework out of the way before dinner. He'd be free, then, for his computer games, or whatever.

As she worked, Gail was envisioning just how she was going to set up the dinner table. She knew she would use those candlesticks! And as she sprinted about, she was feeling excited. This meal was going to be special.

She opted for a favorite no-iron, peach-colored tablecloth, and picked up the matching napkins, arranging the 4 place settings. Stirring the chicken pieces as she went by, she switched off the wok. A few minutes before serving time, she would add the bag of prepared stir-fry vegetables. And tonight, she would add fresh mushroom slices along with some slivered water chestnuts from her pantry supply.

Tonight, for some reason, she just felt extra good, and she wanted to share it!

Gingerly, she picked up the 3 candlesticks from where she'd left them on the kitchen counter, taking them to the table. As she walked by Ethan, he asked, "Whatcha got there, Mom?"

Smiling at him, she answered, "Ethan, these are candlesticks, and they are very special. When I went to the front door to get the mail, there was a package from an old aunt of mine in Illinois, and these were in it." Then she added, "These are very old. Just think, they've been made out of the wood from a table that an old relative, another Ethan, made a long time ago, 'way back in 1850'."

To that, young Ethan said, "Wow!" Then he asked, "Is that where you got my name? From that old Ethan?"

"No," his mom replied. "Matter of fact, until I got this package I'd never heard of him."

"Mom, why in the world did you ever pick a name like that for me? You coulda called me 'Bill' or 'John'. I woulda liked something decent like that!"

Gail smiled at him, "Because we liked 'Ethan.' It was a good name. Did you know that it comes from the Hebrews, and it means 'strength'?"

"No," Ethan said. He mulled that over for a moment, then he said, "Cool," saying it more for himself than for anyone else. And then he went on with his paper work.

Gail arranged the pretty candlesticks mid-center of the table. They looked so elegant. She could tell that the wood was oak, and the grain was particularly golden.

Going to the hutch drawer where she kept her reserve candle supply, she chose 2 tapers in a shade of lime green, placing them in the shortest and the tallest of the holders. And for the middle candlestick, she chose a pretty cranberry one.

Next she picked some soft peach silk flowers, adding a cranberry one here and there for accent, arranging them with a little greenery around the three bases, enhancing the finished look.

Gail stepped back to view what she'd put together.

Shaking her head in approval, she felt satisfied that the table looked just right! No, it was more than looking just right. There was a difference. There was a regal look about it.

She could feel it. Those candlesticks with their oaken grain radiating that lovely luster seemed to command a respect.

Lingering there for a moment, Gail sensed a specialness. She couldn't quite put a finger on it, but, that table area was making her feel good. As if there was a quiet, gentle magnetism about the whole area, and it was making her smile.

Briefly, a car motor sounded, then some rumbling noises of the big garage door going down, and soon the pass through-door opened, all signifying that Bruce was home.

Passing Gail en route to the family room where he'd be setting down his briefcase, he gave her a fond kiss of greeting. Backing off a bit, smiling, "You look all bouncy, or something! What's up?" And then, his eyes sweeping over the table, noting the different look, he said, "Oh, I see, somebody's been shopping!"

"Oh, Bruce, you just can't know how excited I am! When I got home, there was a package at our door. And it was from an old aunt in Illinois. She sent us those old, old candlesticks. Bruce, they are OLD. They've been in the family for years and years.

Gail paused to catch a breath, then went on, "Aunt Molly had a note in the box, and she said we could call her for more information about them. I'm going to phone her tonight!"

Stopping a moment by the table, Bruce looked them over. "Well, I can see they've been well-taken care of, all right. They look nice." With that he went on to the family room to deposit his things.

Bruce, too, had had a demanding day of his own, and now he was in the mood for a nice family evening. And dinner, smelling good, was going to be a pleasant start.

Two

Gail's "Hard-sell" Sales Pitch

"Okay, Aunt Mollie," Gail was saying into the phone. "I'll tell all this to Bruce, and then I'll call you again. I must warn you, though, that Bruce is not much of a traveler. We have a busy life here, always involved with our kids and our friends. I guess we tend to live within our own little world. But, Aunt Mollie, I want you to know, this has been so nice talking with you. We've been on this phone for an hour, I think. I hope you're not worn out!"

To which she heard her aunt say, "On the contrary, Gail. This has been so refreshing. I would love so much for you and your family to come and stay with me for a nice visit. There is so much history here. And you are a part of it, you know. Bruce is just bound to find all this to be interesting, I promise you."

The two soon finished up with their talk, difficult as it was to end it. They each were finding so much to say. Gail had been a small girl when she'd last seen this aunt.

Being born in California where her mother had grown up, Illinois and that part of the relatives had always seemed a long way off. Although Gail's grandfather was born and raised in Illinois, he had settled in the West where his work had taken him.

Shutting off the phone, laying it on the bedside table, for a moment, she just sat there, resting against the bed pillows. But clearly her countenance was reflecting a bustling mind.

Once dinner was over and the kitchen work finished along with Holly's help, Gail had chatted briefly with Bruce. She'd watched him getting settled in the family room with the daily Omaha World Herald and the TV. All the while she'd been anxious to get here in the quiet of their bedroom to make this phone call to her aunt.

Gail was so revved up about all this. What an unexpected evening this had become. But facing her now was the hard part. She had to sell this trip idea to Bruce. This idea of going to Aunt Mollie's in Illinois. Definitely, this would involve some strategy.

Knowing Bruce, already she was well aware of just what his reaction was going to be. He would come out with a great big negative "no."

Truly Bruce was a wonderful guy. He liked doing things with the family, but he was never one to show excitement. He was the very best at being a good father, and he worked diligently at being a good provider. Over the years they'd enjoyed nice vacations, but those mostly had been confined to more local areas. It was only now and then they'd visit with her folks in California.

Sitting there, propped against those pillows, all quiet and comfortable, her mind was reasoning. Mentally she was listing pros and cons involved in making such a trip as this. First and foremost, she had to weigh the facts entailed and decide whether it was feasible, both financially and time-wise.

It was now May and the kids' school would soon be out for the summer. She and Bruce each had time off coming to them. And Gail knew they could afford it.

Actually, if Bruce would agree to staying at Aunt Mollie's farmhouse as she had suggested, the entire trip would not be all that expensive, mainly just food and gasoline for the car. The kids would love the change, she just knew.

Mentally assuring the final feasibility in each of the aspects, Gail was ready to play her little game. And, in comparison with so many of the other so-called "pre-decisions" she'd made throughout the past years of their marriage, she was beginning to feel pretty confident about this one.

In temperament, Bruce and Gail were quite different. But their love for each other was deeply felt, and their individualities had a way of meshing that seemed to make a completeness.

Gail was out-going and fun-loving. And she felt she knew Bruce in and out, and was comfortable in seeming to know what they needed as a family. After all, she had that innate quality of being a good organizer, and reveled in neatly pigeonholing everything in its proper place.

Bruce, on the other hand, was pretty much given to seeing only the black and white of things. He wasn't much for speculation.

Swinging her legs over the side of the bed, shoving her bare feet into her thongs, she sauntered out into the family room.

Bruce was still in his favorite chair, all relaxed with his shoes kicked off and his feet on the big ottoman. His empty coffee mug was setting on the lamp table beside him. It was almost time for the TV's nightly news.

"Bruce, I need a cup of coffee. Can I fill your cup?" she asked him. Quite sure of his answer, already she was picking up the cup. Both of them were coffee lovers.

Returning from the kitchen, setting his steaming cup beside him, Gail settled in her chair angled next to him. Thoughtfully, half-listening to the news commentator, she sat there, sipping her coffee. She knew the news segment had top priority. And this trip thing had to be handled just right.

Also, from habit, she knew that on evenings at home like this, if they weren't involved with a good movie, as soon as the news was over Bruce would turn off the TV. They would chat awhile, winding down, then they'd begin the nightly routine of getting things in order and ready for bed.

Just as expected, as the screen went black, Bruce picked up his coffee mug. Turning to Gail, he smiled, saying, "Well, hello there! What's going on in your department?"

"Well...I just had the best visit over the phone with my Aunt Mollie. You know, Bruce, she brought back some nice memories. I must have been about 5 or 6 years old when my mom and dad and I made the car trip out to Illinois where she lived. We were with my granddad and grandmother."

Gail looked happily lost in her reminiscing. She went on, "It seems like it took us several days to get there from California. But I do remember getting to that big old farm where Grandpa's sister, Mollie, and her family lived. I thought that house was a big castle, and I remember Grandpa said that was where he was born."

Thoughtfully, taking a sip of coffee, Bruce said, "I'll bet that was quite a trip for you. Probably though, being a kid, you're remembering is a bit exaggerated."

"Yes, I know how little kids are. But, not about the house, Bruce. That was real. I remember thinking how lucky Grandpa had been to get to live there and to play there. I still remember that there were so many paths to run on. I just knew it was the wonderful fairyland I'd always read about in my books.

Gail hadn't thought about all that for a long time. Now she knew, more than ever, she wanted to see it again.

Slowly, taking some sips of her coffee, she looked at Bruce, studying him. How was she going to make him see this! Carefully, she began, "Bruce, Aunt Mollie told me that the farm has been occupied by members of our family dating back

15

to the 1860s. That's when our relative, Ethan Bennett, had homesteaded the land, coming there from Ohio. He's the one who had cut down the oak tree from their own forest back there in Ohio. That was in 1850. And those candlesticks out there on our table are made from that same wood. Just think of that, Bruce! And now they're going to be ours!" Gail was fairly beaming.

Sipping his coffee, Bruce had heard everything that she was saying. But, all the while, watching her, he was having some competition going on. His mind was thinking, *Holy gees, she's so beautiful when she's excited and all lit-up like this.* And he could feel his heart doing some flip-flops.

Unmindful of all that, and thinking Bruce's face was reflecting interest in what she was saying, Gail was encouraged. She went on, "My aunt said that down through the years one family member or another had kept journals of the family happenings, and she has all those writings. The first ones date way back to the early 1800s. For some reason, my aunt thinks that our family...you and me, Bruce, and our kids...should be the ones to take them over from her. Can you believe that, Bruce?"

Well no, Bruce couldn't believe that. And he said so in just a few words, ending with, "You know, Gail, I couldn't care less about family genealogy. You've never seen me excited or concerned about any of my family. In fact, for me, the only family that matters is right here in this house. Right here, in Bellevue, Nebraska."

"Yes, I know, Bruce. And our little family here is wonderful. But at times I do get the feeling that we are pretty isolated." She hesitated a moment, then plunged on with what she had to say, "Anyway, Aunt Mollie wants us to come out to her place for a visit. She wants us, personally, to get the feel of the history right where a lot of it was made."

"Oh, no, Gail, absolutely not!" Bruce came out adamantly, definitely alerted to where she was going with this. "We're not traipsing off to any Illinois on any hair-brained wild goose chase venture. You don't know what we'd be getting into. If that old aunt wants you to have any of that stuff, she can box it up and send it to you."

Gail hesitated, looking at him. She smiled at him. Now, this was more like the Bruce she knew. This was the very reaction she had anticipated. And she wasn't the least bit daunted.

Quiet for a while, she sipped some more coffee. She was ready with her next ploy.

Still looking at Bruce, smiling so sweetly, in her very calmest manner, she said, "Okay, then, if you'd rather not go, you don't have to. But, if it's okay with you, the kids and I will go without you. We'll make a real lark of it. As soon as school is out in June, I'll use some of my days coming to me from work. Holly and Ethan will love it."

Then, quickly, she added, "While we are gone, you can use the time to do whatever you'd like…maybe take a few days off yourself…catch up on some golf or something."

Bruce was startled. He couldn't believe what he'd just heard her say. He and Gail had never taken separate vacations in all the years of their marriage. Well, there'd been those few times when one or the other had gone alone to a work-involved conference, but that was different.

He just sat there, not moving. Gail had surprised him. But, one thing he did have to admit. Gail always did know how to make a trip fun, and he couldn't imagine ever letting them go like that without his being a part of it.

Bruce was trapped, and he knew it. He had some backtracking to do. He began with, "Holy gees, Gail, you know I'd worry about you and the kids out there alone on the roads. It's a long way across there to Illinois." Stalling he busied himself with his coffee, watching for her reaction.

Then, he said, "Well, okay. All right. We can go, I guess, although I want you to know I'm dead-set against it. But, I'll take you." He hesitated a moment, then added, "You'll have to attend to all the details. Find out how to get there. But, remember this, we have to stay nights in a motel. No way am I going to be out in any boondocks with some old senile woman. And especially at some old place where we'd have to do without all the things we're used to."

Gail just smiled. Jumping to her feet, she went to him, gently sitting on his lap. Giving him a great big hug, she said, "Bruce, I love you so much. Thank you." Then, "Okay, I'll keep in touch with Aunt Mollie and make all the arrangements. I guarantee that you won't be sorry. I know right now that we are going to have a wonderful time," and she pressed her cheek against his.

Bruce loved her too. Even more so, seeing her beaming so happily as she was right now. After all, Gail was his "right arm," his very best friend. From the very first, she had stood by his side, equally sharing the responsibilities of running their household, and Bruce knew they made a good team.

Right now, though, he did feel a trifle guilty, maybe even a bit jealous, thinking that she even would consider going and having fun with the kids without him. At the moment, Illinois with an old woman in the country sticks was the last place he wanted to go, but he wasn't about to be left out!

Pressing his cheek tighter against hers, he suggested, "What d'ya say, right now, we get things ready for bed?"

With that, Gail got up, and running a finger through the two empty cup handles, she picked them up with one hand.

Folding his papers, picking them up in one hand, Bruce stood up, taking Gail's free hand in his other one. Pulling her closely to him, mischievously, in a low voice, he said very closely to her ear, "Later on, how about your showing me all about some of this love stuff?"

Together, then, they walked toward the kitchen, switching off lights as they went. Reaching the open area, spontaneously, Bruce, with his free hand, again pulled Gail to him. And he kissed her with all the tenderness he was feeling, kissing her in only the way a man truly in love with his mate can embrace.

He released her then, quietly. And he went on to the utility room to deposit the newspaper in the container for recycling.

Gail, left standing there with those coffee mugs dangling on her finger, had to get in control. Her legs were all wobbly. But, of one thing she was sure. She wanted more.

Going on into the kitchen, her feet were barely connecting with the floor. But from routine, almost without thinking, she attended to the coffee maker, getting it ready for the timer to activate in the morning.

Bruce was busy at seeing to getting the house ready for the night.

THREE

Ohio: In The Beginning

The Bennett forest sprawled, surrounding the cleared area abutting the almost perfect glen. A glen that was now dotted with the rugged buildings of the families' homestead.

That forest ever emitted such a peacefulness. Such a quiet loveliness. It covered the many-acre tract of land spreading amongst the rolling hills alongside the blue waters of the Ohio River. And as the river meandered along, it was marking the southern boundary of that land belonging to the Caleb Bennett family there in those early beginning years of the 1800s in the new state of Ohio.

At first, there was just Caleb and Minerva's log home. They'd built it with only one room, setting it solidly and securely on its well-packed dirt floor. And, wisely, Caleb had made the ceiling rafters of logs strong to allow for a future loft, hoping he and his new young wife would be having children.

Along with the house was a barn for their animals. A barn for the team of oxen and a couple of horses. And there was a cow that provided the milk, the cream and the butter.

For Caleb and Minerva, life was not in a hurry in those days, in the beginning. Their little hand-built home of logs was quite adequate even as their first son was born, and then a little girl, or even with a second son and another girl. With them, as was with their few sparsely scattered neighbors; this was the accepted way of the times.

Each scattered neighbor, each an adventurous sort, settlers like Caleb and Minerva, had forged out his own little haven on his own claimed tract. And as each baby addition enlarged the family occupancy, each day's work had merely expanded to meet the added necessities. Like more bread to bake, and a bigger garden space to clear and to plant and to tend.

By 1820 a fifth baby had joined that Bennett household, and that fifth child was a boy whom they called Ethan. And by now, the barn had been made double in size, as well as a larger barn had been added. The need for more cows as well as more workhorses made this a necessity, and the harsh Ohio winters demanded shelter.

In back of the barns, a cleared pasture area where the animals grazed was marked off by split rail fencing for containing them.

During this gradual expansion Caleb had good help. At very young ages those young sons of his became adept at working with their father. As they developed in physique, equally did they develop in their pride of Bennett family entitlement. This was evident in the work they turned out each day.

Also during this gradual expansion, the realization had come to Caleb of his need for a small mill to help in making his own lumber for all this early building. And it was this need that fostered the creation of his Bennett Lumber Mill. With Caleb's inherent ability in the overall planning of the best functional design for that Bennett complex, he set the mill nearby the river. There it would be accessible to a waterway as well as being close by to the family home.

Also it was near to where the trees were standing pristine and tall. The trees spread out from the three sides of his nestled grassy glen. And also, Caleb was envisioning what it could be like as his boys neared that inevitable stage of being marriageable.

Those lads were fast outgrowing their father's home. In Caleb's heart he hoped each would want to choose a spot in that very glen to build a log home of his own. He wanted them to remain a part of that little stronghold. He could feel that the boys loved it there as much as he and their mother did.

So the mill was built, and it served the family's needs. But as soon as the news of Caleb's mill spread, that little mill also became a business. Steadily it had to be enlarged as the business grew with other settlers learning of and noting the convenience of their availability of already-sawed boards.

Gradually Caleb had cleared the woods here and there to allow his making of a wagon road leading to the north, junctioning with an east/west more traveled trail. On this trail, to the east a bit, a stagecoach stopover and Trading Post had been set up and it had begun to prosper and enlarge.

In the beginning, that little stopover had been set up out of necessity. With the coming of darkness at each nightfall, horses required feeding and rest. So when stagecoaches began to make sporadic runs, similar stops had begun to spring into being to accommodate this need.

As trails gradually became better marked from usage, the little log stopover structures began dotting along these trails. And they were being strategically placed at spots the length of an average day's travel.

Gradually, as stage business had increased and runs had become more regular, the needs of the travelers were met with expanding facilities. Trading Posts were offering wider selections of supplies. It was only natural that a little community gradually would crop up around such a growing atmosphere.

So, as life happened, the Bennett homestead also flourished and gradually began to fill the grassy glen. And life was good.

The young fruit trees that Caleb and Minerva had set out in the beginning were producing fruit. The woods were full of berries, even a gooseberry bush was growing here and there.

As the two older sons aged, they did get married. And just as Caleb had hoped for, two more log homes were added in the clearing. The gardens got bigger, and each household had its own root cellar to fill. As the older daughter grew, she too was married and still another log home was built. The young groom was content to work with the Bennett's in the mill.

The other daughter, the fourth child, called Carrie, never married. She continued to live with Minerva and Caleb. Even when still quite young, her pair of capable hands happily began to ease the heavy workload of her mother.

FOUR

Growing Up in Early 1800

In 1820 when Caleb and Minerva had been blessed by the birth of that fifth baby, the boy they called Ethan, that little household was full to its log rafters with family and family gear. But with its orderly management it was a most happy and pleasant haven, setting there as it was, all nestled so serenely.

The stately beauty of the woods, protective as it was, gave a sense of richness. This whole aura was even further enhanced by the meandering river that was so close nearby and flowing along bordering the Bennett glen.

As Caleb's sons had grown, getting huskier and stronger, they'd become invaluable aids at their father's side, making all this gradual progress possible. But, somehow, from the very beginning, it was felt that the youngest boy, Ethan, always seemed somewhat special. As he grew and developed, his older siblings responded to his warm, sensitive personality, making it easy for them to treat him with favoritism.

Nevertheless, even though he was being allowed this somewhat more privileged childhood than had his older siblings known, Ethan was just as thoroughly being taught all the basic necessities for the hard survival of livelihood in that day and time. Not only did he learn, but he also was required to perform his share. Thus, like his brothers, he became a strong and healthy young man.

But, even as a young child, tending to the simple chores that were allotted to him and then the heavier tasks that became his responsibility as he had his birthdays, Ethan displayed a tenderness. A gentleness. This quality flowed out from him, subtlely, instinctively. The animals felt it. The family felt it.

Carrie always felt it, bonding closely with her young brother. But Carrie, with all the constant laborious household work, never had too much time beyond practicality.

Time, that is, until the family's evenings. Time, at last, when each task for that day had been completed, and the darkness of night had settled over the glen. It was then they gathered inside that one main room of their little home.

It was here in that crowded, although adequate, one room where the family cooked and ate. Where they sat. Where they bathed. And where in one curtained-off corner, was Caleb and Minerva's bed.

The children's beds were now in the loft. Early on, with the setting up of the mill, Caleb had created the loft under the cabin roof.

Laboriously, he had made that floor, supporting it well for the rough usage he knew it would get when the children would climb up to their beds. For accessing the loft, Caleb had left a gaping hole in the floor about midway of the one wall end. He then had built a makeshift ladder, attaching it onto that wall, starting at the ground level of the room below and extending up through the hole in the loft floor.

So, with the coming of each nightfall, it was in this one ground-level room where the family members would gather.

With their glass globes sparkling after each day's cleaning, the coal oil lamps did their best to light the little portions of space where the activities were taking place. And from the early days of fall, through the long bitter cold of the winters and on into the chilliness of late springtime, logs would be kept burning in the big, open fireplace. Caleb had built the fireplace as a part of the wall opposite the one with the ladder.

So it was here each evening that the family members sat, discussing happenings of the day, or making plans for work for tomorrow. Or they just rested and comfortably enjoyed each other's company. The solidity of the little family haven, the pleasantness emanating through the warmth and the crackling of the open fire, made for contentment.

Even the black darkness of the night encircling just beyond the log walls emitted a peacefulness that gave comfort. It signified a welcome time for rest, giving a feeling of completeness, nestled as they were in their cleared spot there in the forest.

And if there was a necessity for going out into that darkness, like for trips to the "outhouse," or tending to the animals, a lantern was always available.

Minerva's hands would be busy with her basket of mending, or her needlework. She would have made sure that the dough for tomorrow's bread was resting there in its floured spot in the well-worn wooden dough box all covered and waiting.

And young Carrie, completely unknowing of any scholarly talent she was blessed with, dutifully sat at one end of the big, homemade kitchen table. Almost nightly, she would jot down the day's happenings, even sometimes throwing in a morsel of observation of her own.

Sitting there, writing, Carrie emitted a look of specialness. Her rough calloused fingers would be holding her treasured feather quill pen, with her bottle of black ink setting nearby. She regarded that ink as a luxury, sensing a caring and a kindness in her father for buying her such a lavish gift. It made her feel very special, and she was very careful to not waste it or spill it.

Ethan loved watching Carrie. He had watched her do this for as long as he could remember. With yellowish parchment paper spread before her, she would dip the sharpened point of the quill into the inkbottle. Then, soberly, thoughtfully, she would write.

The middle of that table was always full, but always it was tidy and clean. There were the usual condiments and jars of homemade pickles. There were the jars of relishes and jams. Now, each jar or jelly glass was lidded after the cleaning of its rim as part of the clean-up ritual following each meal. There was a little toothpick holder, filled for use. The sugar bowl, and the spoon holder were setting there, refilled, that too a part of that daily after-meal cleaning ritual.

A part of this after-meal ritual included taking careful stock of any nearly empty jars. Then, on the trip to the root cellar for bringing any necessary supplies needed in preparing for the next meal, replacements for these would be taken care of.

The accomplishment of that amassed store in the root cellar was a source of great pride and feelings of thankfulness in the women of the households. Those neat rows of Mason jars displayed anything in vegetables, meats and fruits that could be found living or growing, either in the garden or in the woods. And from each falltime harvest were the root crops. These were laying in shallow piles for drying.

Anything that would make a cobbler or a pie or a stew was preserved and stored and considered a blessing.

During the warmer weather seasons any victual leftovers would have been taken down to the cool springhouse. Here they would be setting on the specially chosen flat-topped rocks that Caleb had placed here and there in the cool spring water that flowed through the springhouse.

Setting there too would be the home-churned butter. It would be in its lidded stoneware crock. Setting nearby would be the smaller meal-sized butter dish. Near the back door of the family house, attached to the outside wall, Caleb had built a high ledge shelf. During the colder Ohio weather, some leftover foods were placed out there, tightly covered of course.

High as it was, the larger animals, foraging at night, couldn't get to it. The little critters who could scurry up that logged wall, like the squirrels and raccoons, were no match for those heavy iron pot lids. Or for the rocks anchoring the ironstone dinner plates that were sometimes used as lids on those stone crocks.

Setting there, when the weather was at a lower freezing temperature, that food was only the better preserved.

Caleb was so thankful for that natural cool spring water bubbling out from that wooded hillside that bordered his homestead site on the east.

Knowing of the spring's value he'd opted to build his and Minerva's log home near its vicinity. Mother Nature had already provided him with the lush, level, grassy glen in this spot of his forest.

Amid the myriad of other projects that had faced Caleb in getting all the demands of the living quarters set up, during the intervals whenever he could find the time, he had designed and laboriously built the little springhouse.

He had gathered flat rocks, chinking them together with a mud made from clay to make the walls. This spring, of course, was the natural source of the water supply for the Bennett household. It was ever cool, ever healthful, and ever flowing.

And by channeling a flow from the spring through his rock house structure, then placing several flat-topped stones here and there in that channel, Caleb had the ideal place for setting foods for cooling.

For keeping animals out, he'd built a makeshift gate that temporarily could be set aside and out of the way. Animals could drink from other spots along the little spring-fed brook that meandered on its way down to the river.

How refreshing, walking through that shaded entry, hearing the pleasant soft babbling coming from the water hitting against the stones as it flowed. Such a woodsy smell! It was so nice to get cooled by that atmosphere, and even more so by drinking that water, using that always-available tin cup. For a moment, a man could feel so rich! Such an uplifting for a work-tired body!

By now, there was a well-worn path from the back door of the cabin to that springhouse. Along with another well-worn path to the root cellar that Caleb had dug into that hillside. Here those reserved glass jars of canned foods along with the piles of potatoes and onions, the apples and other fruits, were protected from the freezing cold of the Ohio winters.

Making trip after trip along these paths was an accepted routine. Accepted just as were all the chores required in tending to the many daily needs revolving around the lives of a caring household.

Like now, here at the table where Carrie was sitting, at each family member's usual place lay his refolded cloth napkin, all ready for use at the next meal.

These napkins were hand made and were reused from meal to meal, until they became too soiled. Then clean, ironed ones were always ready to replace them. And used those napkins were, three meals a day, every day, there at that table, except for occasional special Sabbaths.

Occasionally, when the traveling preacher could be in their vicinity, on a Sabbath, in good weather, there would be an all day "gathering" at the little community Trading Post.

Getting to attend this little gathering would always be an exciting event. It was a break in the everyday routine. Participating in the gathering gave a brief tangible touch with the outside world.

The Trading Post was like a little oasis. Here stood a rambling log structured building. Here the family of the scattered settlers could purchase from a limited supply of items. Items that included things from staples to tack to yard goods for sewing. And, credit could be gotten for hay or eggs or some garden produce.

Also, here where the stagecoach made a stop, the drivers would bring bits of news from the world outside. And there were the paid fares with their contributions of interest. Or some cherished mail for some area family.

Too, any out-going mail from this area would be picked up by a stage driver to begin its risky trek to its destination.

At the trading Post, there were overnight accommodations for stagecoach people, as well as any needed attention for the animals. Getting in off that sometimes perilous wagon trail was always a welcomed opportunity for both the humans and the animals.

The traveling preacher did his commuting on horseback. He would spend his nights bedded down in his own chosen primitive campsite. That would be any likely available spot that would give him some needed water for a little bit of cooking, for filling his water canteen, and sometimes for a bath. Like alongside a brook, a pond, or, sometimes, by a larger stream. Then maybe he would feel awarded by catching a fish or two for frying over his open fire.

His personal gear would be toted in a bag or two, consisting only of a few simple basics. Like something to cook in and a light bed roll for his sleeping. Or when finding a settler's home, he would stop, enjoying the welcoming that he hoped he would receive.

When traveling in areas that he frequented routinely, he would be acquainted with the settlers. There, most often, he would be looked upon as a trusted news carrier, and he would be respected as a man of God.

His horse also would like the welcoming at a friendly home. It would mean being put up in a barn and being treated to some oats and hay.

Once he arrived at a community center, he would stay awhile, letting word get around that there would be a "gathering." There the traveling preacher always was a welcomed visitor. News of a "gathering" was a meaningful social event, never failing to stir excitement.

FIVE

On Becoming a Man

On these Bennett family evenings, Ethan would often watch his sister Carrie, while his own mind would be rampant with boyish dreams.

With the older siblings shouldering much of the parents' work load, their mother, Minerva, somewhat schooled herself, had been able to spend a bit more time with Carrie and Ethan. Those two younger ones benefited from this. Ethan, in his early growing years, benefited even more so than Carrie. And those two were always avid students, inquisitive and eager to learn.

Through his parents' few books, a world outside his small, closed-in Ohio complex was opened up to Ethan, and he found it fascinating.

Carrie liked the concept of written records for preservation of family histories. And to keep an on-going log of Bennett history became her mission.

Ethan would tease Carrie. He'd chide her about the possibility of his someday getting to read a book written by her. But Carrie, knowing of the physical energy required just to get through her day's work, merely scoffed at him. In her mind, that goal would never be an option. A plain ordinary girl from a lumber mill family just couldn't conceive of anything like that.

Ethan on the other hand, was given to daydreaming. He was guilty of this even while he was going about his work. And if this daydreaming, now and then, slowed some of his chore out-put, the family over-looked it. After all, he was the baby, and anyway, he always proved himself to be quite dependable in any responsibility that he was given. To his methodical older brothers, Ethan was like sunshine in their existence.

That never failed in seeming to lighten their load. They never tired of looking out for him. Despite any formal training, the two older brothers seemed to be quite content with their lives there on the family homestead. After all, they'd had a levelheaded, God fearing father like Caleb to follow as their example. They displayed this as they put in a productive day's work.

Once those older brothers were grown, married, and heading up households of their own, right there as a part of that homestead, each could go to his own place each evening, happily counting his own blessings.

Each of those sons, along with the older sister, had limited acquaintance with the "three R's." But from birth each had shown a natural ability for good reasoning. Working with Caleb, with the lumber, with all the building, with the measuring, each had become remarkably adept in that "R" category designating 'rithmatic. So the aura emitted by each of them was one of comfortable contentment. A contentment sparked from a happy, confident individual. An individual void of any doubt of his ability to cope with even the most stressful of situations that often arose in those rugged times.

Ethan loved his family. He too was mindful of blessings, and this awareness gave him compassion. As he was advancing through his years of puberty into his boyish years of early manhood, he looked forward to those Sabbath times of the "gatherings" at the Trading Post center.

Amongst the other settlers' families that would be attending, there would always be some boys around Ethan's age. Never bashful, it was easy for him to draw them out in conversation. And, more often than not, as the boys were beginning to show maturity, the girls of those families started to join in with the boys' group. And the boys began to allow that to happen.

As expected, there would be the usual bantering and teasing. But right from that first Sabbath Day that Ethan had spotted her, there was one girl that was different from the others. Ethan never joined the other boys in teasing her. Right from the start, he had the strange feeling that he wanted to protect her.

It didn't take too many "gatherings" for Ethan to learn some things about this girl. For one thing, she had a most beautiful name, RoseMarie. That name seemed to lilt off Ethan's lips like a lovely song. And more and more, as Ethan went about his chores, that lovely name kept lilting off his lips, over and over. Quietly, of course. But he knew. And he was taking notice that the whole world seemed to be smiling all about him! But, he kept all this to himself. He himself didn't want to be teased.

Now, Ethan never minded being teased by his siblings, but he didn't want there to be any teasing about RoseMarie. And he just couldn't bear sharing with anyone the unbelievably delicious thoughts he was having about that girl. He almost was afraid even to think about such a thing, really, but it seemed like, just maybe, she was acting as though she liked him.

These things were all so new to Ethan. Sure, he knew about love and being loved, but he had never known about love feelings like this.

Before long he learned that her parents lived and worked right there at the Trading Post. Her mother was a cook and her father was one of the tenders of the animals. Also, RoseMarie was about his age. She'd been born in 1821, just one year after his own birth in 1820.

To Ethan, RoseMarie got prettier with each "gathering" time. And whenever his father, or maybe an older brother, hitched up a team to drive into the settlement, if his own work allowed it, he finagled somehow to be on the wagon to go along. Even now and then, he would be the one to be sent by himself. But any such trip to the Trading Post was sporadic. The family livelihood was maintained fairly self-sufficiently right there within their own little glen.

With the rows of glass jars in the root cellars filled with the summer's garden vegetables or with the home-canned fruits from the trees or bushes bearing them, each good meal was assured. Then there were the piles of potatoes dug each fall, and the eating apples in the barrels.

With the flour and the sugar at the Trading Post in 100-pound cloth bags and the salt packed in 5-pound cloth sacks, those settlement trips were necessary only now and then.

However, it was beginning to be noticeably evident to Ethan that RoseMarie truly was responding to the attention he'd been showing her. And, for sure, it was at that very realization when, miraculously, his every day world, the one in which he'd been existing, became utterly transformed, unbelievably and wonderfully so.

At once, that day-to-day little world, almost always mostly confined to that little glen, suddenly took on a magical hue. An incredibly marvelous world it was, bringing with it such a mixture of feelings. The kind of feelings that made Ethan feel special. His already warm and compassionate, tender traits seemed to compound.

Ethan Bennett was in love! With a girl!

If only Ethan could have known, these traits would continue to radiate from him for as long as he would draw a breath.

It's these very feelings that base the ingredients that make up utopias. And utopias have been ever present and a part of our Master's overall creation plan. All heaven must smile when a man with his mate, declaring such profound love for each other, steps into his very own utopia.

In a true utopia, man together with his household ever becomes an enhancement to the Big Creation in general. And somehow, such a utopia never ceases to be sprinkled with favors.

Unaware as he was, Ethan was destined to have and to share just such a utopia.

SIX

Wedding Bells for Ethan

Ethan awakened.

Already the loft was lighted dimly by the coming dawn. But, Ethan's mind told him it was still too early in the morning. He just wasn't ready yet to roll out of bed.

Slowly, he stretched out the length of his body, and then settled in again, putting his hands behind his head on his pillow.

It was almost June, and the early summer's warmth was feeling good. Just think, here it was, already well into 1837! And, somehow, already, he'd gotten to be seventeen! Seventeen years of strong, sturdy muscle building. Ethan harbored no doubts but that he was a full-grown man.

Today was Saturday. But it was no ordinary Saturday. Tomorrow was the Sabbath, and there was going to be a community "gathering" at the Trading Post. So today was going to be a busy day for the whole Bennett clan. There was lots of extra work to be done so they'd each be ready to attend that "gathering" in full swing!

Work like getting the hubs of the wagon wheels greased. Packing noontime feed and some hay to take along for the horses. All the harness had to be inspected. And, the ladies in the houses would have the foods to prepare for the baskets. And they'd have to see that the Sabbath clothes were clean and in order, and any missing buttons replaced. The Sabbath shoes would have to be checked, maybe polished and shined up a bit. Oh, yes indeed, today was going to be busy all right!

And RoseMarie! She would be there. She'd be all prettied-up.

Anticipation of that brought smiles that brightened Ethan's little curtained cubicle!

Outside, the morning noises had begun. A rooster crowed. A cow or two gave out a familiar bawl making it known they were ready to be milked. And in her own little curtained off bed space, there in her part of the loft, his older sister, Carrie, was breathing deeply and rhythmically.

It was then that Ethan could hear his father and mother stirring below.

Privacy for family members in a one-room-with-loft house was almost nonexistent, and Ethan had grown to his young manhood with that. Now, with the two older brothers and his older sister married and in their own homes there in the glen, there was more personal space. But, even so, acoustics didn't warrant a whole lot of secrecy.

Minerva had taught respect and decency amongst the children, and bathing was managed behind a curtained off area…near a wood burning stove during cold months. Being clad in one's underwear was accepted as being "decent" during the scurrying around, "getting ready" times.

So, overhearing his folks talk was just a normal thing. Ethan and the others had grown up with that.

Ethan didn't intend to listen. But evidently his father was feeling his own excitement with thoughts about the "gathering." It wasn't his usual bed-related muffled tones that were wafting up to the loft and to Ethan's ears. Ethan couldn't believe what he was hearing.

His father was talking in such a different manner, more like a teasing tone. Ethan could hear him saying, "and now, my pretty little lady, you just lay right here. I'm going to get that fire going in that kitchen stove, and then…and then-n-n...I'm-a comin' right back here...and then, my pretty little lady...I'm gonna use you!"

Ethan was shocked! His father's words were sort of muffled-like, but, clearly, they were not muffled enough!

Ethan felt funny...he felt odd! He felt guilty, like he'd just trespassed. He pulled the light summer-weight blanket up over his ears. He didn't want to hear any more!

A moment passed. Then, man that he was, Ethan became quite thoughtful, even began to smile at himself. After all, wasn't that the way he himself had come about getting into this world? He'd grown up being around the animals. He knew all about animal husbandry. And, naturally, he'd dealt with his own male adolescence. But these days were different. Now, there was a girl in Ethan's picture. And he was in love with that girl. He wanted to be close to her. He'd rather be near her than in any other place.

In fact, these days he'd been thinking more about him and RoseMarie than anything else. And he was just sure that she was acting like she wanted to be near him just as well.

He'd even begun wondering, actually, just what it would be like to kiss her! And when imaging that, if he happened to be standing up at such a moment, thinking like that, his legs would get all wobbly. Like all the starch had gone out of them.

Ethan pulled down the cover. He shifted his body position, settling in comfortably. He began to grin, impishly. He was thinking, and visualizing, *"what if RoseMarie was laying here in bed beside me right now! We'd be married! Oh, man, would I ever be kissing those pretty lips of hers right now...,"* and Ethan got all awash with a warm and happy and a feel-good all over.

Always, when he'd been with the group of boys at the "gatherings" as they'd grown older, he'd hear their talk. Talk about what they'd like to do with a girl. But to Ethan, the way they said it, it always had sounded dirty. And as he'd begun more and more to get this liking for pretty RoseMarie, he'd never had any thoughts associated with her that would in any way violate that lovely girl. All he wanted was to hold her close. He wanted to love her, and to protect her.

Sure, every part of him was aching to have her lying there beside him. Right now, this morning, especially, he wanted that more than ever. Imagine, exploring the marriage act together, he and his RoseMarie.

Just thinking about it, a flood of warm, all melty-like, all golden-like feeling again washed through him...oh, how he loved that girl...

Suddenly, Ethan became dead still... *"Oh, my God! Oh... my God...that's what I want. I'm going to ask RoseMarie if she wants that! I've got to build a house...I'm going to marry her."*

Suddenly, he sat straight up in bed! He was certain! *"Yes sir, I am ready to get married...I am ready to build a house of my own...I'm going to talk to my father,"* and, in his mind, he was so adamant about it, he'd come close to voicing it right out loud!

SEVEN

Perforating Boundaries

It had been in the very early 1800s, around 1808, when Caleb and Minerva Bennett had heard about this newly opened territory called Ohio. Leaving their homeland in Pennsylvania as young newlyweds, their wagon was so well packed with love and exuberance that any lack in personal gear was trivial. On reaching the new state, and after days of travel, they had chosen their spot, settling on it, getting it established as a claim of their own.

At the very first, when they had come upon this section of forest, they'd known they had found their perfect place. Settling in, they had acknowledged the few other scattered homesteaders that already were living there on their own claims. And, like those others, they had busied themselves, concentrating on homemaking.

As other pioneering families happened along, liking the area, they too would claim neighboring space. Before long, a self-contained little community had taken shape within its own limited bounds. Such a setting, hard bent on daily existence, was not conducive to being in touch with any outside worldly goings on.

With all the unexplored virgin land beckoning, slowly, yet quite steadily, many were the families crisscrossing, on the move, searching for new opportunities. Here and there, in isolated areas, little communities much like that of the Bennett's had begun to dot the landscapes.

Such a community would thrive, quite contentedly, resulting in its becoming a small marooned environment

With this flux of movement as more and more people were pursuing their dreams, gradually, the old wagon trails were becoming well-marked roads. Soon, in meeting the demands of travelers, stagecoach runs were becoming regular and dependable. This in turn created the need and opportunity for more stage stopovers with Trading Posts.

With an ever-increasing variety of new products being offered and stocked at the Trading Posts along the routes, there was also a steady growth in the business of hauling.

In Caleb and Minerva's area, with rolling hills, following closely along the big river, the land travelers found it easier to drive more inland, wending along the grassy flats. Thus, with the passing of each year, that main wagon trail running east/west to the north of their settlement had become a well packed-down thoroughfare.

Like the other trails, it was now smooth with the earth having hardened from such continuous use. In these days, with the settlers noting the change, remarks were often made that it would take a heavy drenching rain before the wagons would make those deep, black muddy ruts like in the olden days!

Still, it was only when needed staples were running low that a settler would leave his tiny complex to make the drive to the Trading Post. But on those infrequent trips, there were noticeably more and more bits of news from the outside to be picked up. News brought in by stage drivers and by wayfarers stopping in. They told of things going on in a changing world outside the little isolated compound.

From time to time a traveler would bring stories about all the new territories that had opened up. Word was that the territory abutting Ohio on the west of them was made into a state that was called Indiana. That had occurred in 1816.

Then the news was being told that the land along the west side of that new Indiana was given statehood as well, and this territory was named Illinois. That had happened in 1818.

On the hearing of this information, it was becoming apparent to the settlers that there was getting to be quite a growing country outside their little complex. They were made aware that life as they had known in those earlier years had indeed undergone a state of change.

Inadvertently, with learning about and discussing all this information about constant growth, some mind-expanding was going on within the Bennett's own little family as well as with their neighbors.

Imaginations were being triggered in the minds of those locals. Most of them had never been further away than their own Trading Post area since their migration from the east. Or, for that matter, with their lacking in book learning, they'd never heard of or thought about places beyond their own settlement. For the most part, though, there was a great interest and an eagerness to learn more.

Within Caleb's little glen, with the family talk about these newsy happenings, a flood of personal memories would well up in Caleb and Minerva. And, of course, their growing family liked to hear the tales of the older folks' adventures.

Caleb and Minerva would tell stories of the different emotions they'd experienced during their earlier years as youths back in Pennsylvania in about 1808. Back when they too had begun to hear the talk about opportunities in the new state of Ohio. That event of statehood had occurred a few years previously in 1803.

They'd been young. They were still courting. But even now, as they told about it, Caleb and Minerva would still feel some of their old tremendous excitement.

Back then, as they had heard talk about how easy it was to stake a claim, they had made their decision that they too wanted to get their start in this new land. They'd done a lot of dreaming about it. So they'd gotten married and said good-bye to Pennsylvania and their families.

How shocked their parents had been when those two young people had begun loading up their few belongings. But now, when telling about it, they dared to admit that once they actually had gotten miles along their way, that trek into the unknown had suddenly begun to loom as being quite wild. That new territory, at times, had suddenly seemed so very far away.

But, bravely, even through those uncertain moments, they had kept on. They'd kept heading west, just the two of them with their few supplies, sitting on that wagon seat, with the reins to their pair of oxen in Caleb's strong young hands. But their love for each other was never lacking, and their big dream kept them sustained.

And that's how they'd found this haven of their own, here by the river. That had been a few years back, in 1808 or '09.

Now, clearly, big changes were taking place. The days were gone when each little settler complex was a family oriented, self-contained tiny community of its own. Gone were those old days when a trip to the Trading Post was made only when the list of needs was lengthy. Now such trips were no longer considered to be an occasion.

Also, it was a fact that while the little Bennett complex boundaries were being penetrated from the outside, there was change as well taking place from within.

While the confines of the little settlement were being inundated with all this knowledge from the fast-growing world outside, the reputation of Bennett's Lumber Mill was spreading out. Now, it wasn't just the locals who were taking advantage of the availability of the lumber and wood products. There was an ever-increasing proof of a wider clientele being attested by the loaded wagons busy on the trails. This was evidenced also in the bundles of wood tied onto rafts or secured in flat boats maneuvering on the river.

Even the river itself was changing. It was becoming quite noisy with traffic. Where there once had been occasional travelers in flat boats or on rafts made of logs, now there were getting to be big-sized paddle boats, some coming, it was said, from as far away as a place called St. Louis.

And all this fresh news brought in by the river boat people and by stagecoach drivers and passengers was like hearing about a new far-off world. The news was breathtaking. Awesome. It was exciting. Some of it was even scary.

An ambitious man, with his family, could choose a spot and set about to make a dream grow into a reality. And if that dream was in the fertile mind of an opportunist, his choice for such a spot likely would be on the bank of a good river or alongside a wagon trail that showed a promising potential.

Once his choice spot was decided upon, the man with his family would set up a beginning business. Then, with the exercising of some appealing ingenuity, the spot was rife with opportunity for fast growth. And from there it would be only natural that out of the increasing traffic of transients, both by river craft and on the wagon trails, certain ones would want to put their own talents into businesses of their choosing. This would result, almost overnight, in the mushrooming of a little town.

According to the talk of the passers-by, population was increasing year by year. In part, this was due to the migration coming from the eastern original states, with people of varied nationalities heading out to the new territories and settling in. It was then in natural order that numbers of new babies were appearing in the households of these busy new settlers.

Along with this increase in travelers, among them, now and then, would be some coming from great distances. With their stopping off at the Trading Post, or even docking their watercraft at the Bennett mill if they were taking the river route, they'd have information about the goings on in places much farther away. Such news was fascinating as well as being mind broadening.

With the steady increase of wayfarers coming now, Bennett's forest glen was absorbing the information of places that until now had been unbeknown to that little community; places actually not too far distant that had been established and developing for several years. Like across the end of the state not too far east from them was a growing port on the Ohio River called Cincinnati.

And there was talk of another busy river port at a far away place called New Orleans. Travelers said it was south and west, and located at the end of the big Mississippi River.

Clearly, they were learning of opportunities heretofore unheard of that were now abounding in all of this new land.

What an exciting time to be alive and to be a part of it all! And taking all this news in stride, even the far off state of Indiana began to seem closer.

Learning about all this information was indeed fascinating. Like hearing the stories about an opportunist named Major John Sprinkle.

John, with his wife Susanna and their two children, also had left Pennsylvania. Much like the Bennetts, the Sprinkles were undertaking their own adventure. His mother and father were with them also. This was even before Caleb and Minerva had begun their jaunt back in 1808 or '09.

John Sprinkle and his family were traveling down the Ohio River in a flat boat, and they had tarried for a time along the state of Kentucky side. But with what they saw across on the other side being more appealing, in 1803, in the flatboat, Major Sprinkle crossed the river, then chose a spot on which to settle down.

He set up a blacksmith shop there on a hillside overlooking the river. And, as with the Bennetts, others began to come, and soon a growing settlement was established.

By 1810 Major Sprinkle had obtained a license from the Court of Common Pleas in a community to the north of him called Vincennes. This license allowed John to establish a ferry for crossing the river from his land over to the opposite bank in Kentucky.

Then a couple of years later, John went back to Vincennes. On this trip, he used a log raft. To get to Vincennes, first he went west a bit on the Ohio River, then he rafted up north to his destination on the river called the Wabash. There at the Territorial Land Office he obtained two land grants. Each of these grants was signed by the president of the United States, James Monroe.

Using one of the grants, John had his fast growing community surveyed and he named it Sprinklesburg. Shortly after that his second grant was used for officially forming another nearby growing settlement that was named Mount Prospect.

In 1816 this territory, which included the land where these growing settlements were flourishing, was made into the state that was called Indiana. Then, as with the other new states, it was divided up into counties.

John's town of Sprinklesburg was in Warrick County, and John had the distinction of having formed the first town in that county.

With the passing of the years, Sprinklesburg had expanded with growth, becoming a fast-thriving town. Along the river in that area, there was an era of prosperity and well being. And, back east at the Bennett's settlement, wayfarers traveling from that Indiana area were proud to let that be known.

A stagecoach stop-over and Trading Post called Boonville had been established a few miles to the north of John's town, and in a very short time it had become a busy, well-settled community.

By 1833, Major Sprinkle's Sprinklesburg was becoming known as "the metropolis of southern Indiana." As a thriving river port, business continued to boom.

Farmers around the Boonville area needed to get their crops and produce down to the river which was a distance of about 10 miles. So, the area's first "paved road" was built from

Sprinklesburg up to Boonville. How wayfarers loved to brag about that!

This novel 10-mile thoroughfare became known as "the plank road," and was aptly named since it was built of wooden planks that were laid side to side. Farmers paid a toll to travel on it. Word was that the plank road was crowded daily with folks traveling back and forth.

In 1837 Sprinklesburg was renamed, becoming the town of Newburgh, and news of its constant growth was always followed with interest.

In 1842 the Delaney Academy was founded there, making Newburgh a college town. News began to circulate that the Academy was a Presbyterian school for the training of ministers and teachers.

It was a two-room frame building with a basement. The talk was that the Academy held two sessions a year, each session lasting for five months. The cost was $5.00 to $10.00 a session, and good boarding with private families in the area was available from $1.25 to $1.50 a week.

On hearing this, Ethan Bennett began imagining that some day his own young Carrie would be a likely candidate for just such a school as that Delaney Academy.

One day in 1848 a riverboat traveler tied up at the dock at the Bennett mill. He needed to stretch his legs and ask if he could fill his fresh water containers. During the usual exchange of conversation, he was showing the Bennetts his copy of a newspaper that he'd been carrying. The paper was called "The Chronicle." And he told them he'd purchased it back in Warrick County, Indiana. That was where it was printed. The traveler said he'd gotten the paper when he'd stopped at Newburgh, Indiana, to stock up with supplies.

The Bennetts were quite impressed. They scanned that paper in amazement. Never had they, or any of the other bystanders in the mill, ever before seen a newspaper.

EIGHT

News in the 1850s

By the 1850s accounts were coming in regularly of really far-off lands called California and Oregon. And the stories trickling in about these places were fascinating.

By this time, with more and more families migrating in search of tracts of new land for homesteading, methods of travel were becoming a business. It was becoming a trend for families to pay to be a part of an organized party with an overseer guide to lead them across miles of strange country to their goal.

Also families now were traveling in wagons that were covered. These were wagons built to give some protection from the weather. There was a top covering over a wood-framed support. The covering was made of a white waterproofed material that was called a tarp. And the wagon had a solid wood floor that served to float on the water whenever there was a river that had to be crossed.

Many of these stories, especially if they came through the lips of a florid taleteller, could be most frightening, often downright chilling, especially if the listener happened to be tenderhearted or a child. But to a rugged man, on hearing of the adventures, there would be a stirring of excitement, maybe even a little envy.

That was the case with the tales brought in about all the gold that was being discovered in that land away out west called California in 1848 and '49. The gold was being found in mines in rough mountainous territory, where again, a man could stake out a claim for himself. With a visit to the land office for recording it, legally the claim would be his. He was free, then, to dig for the ore. The gold seekers were dubbed "prospectors."

Or nuggets of gold could be found in the streams amongst the rocks that washed down from those mountain areas. And the stories making news across the country back to the east recounted how a man, using a flat pan, could scoop up a pan full of the rocks. He would shake them around, sorting, and often, luckily, he would see nuggets of gold amidst those rocks. The assayers' offices were kept swamped with evaluating and weighing.

Through someone's ingenuity, screens were used to replace the solid bottoms of the pans. The screen made it easier and faster for the water to drain from the scooped up pan fulls, making the shaking around and the sorting easier. This procedure was termed as "panning for gold!"

Stories were that, in those early days, many prospectors were becoming wealthy overnight. Those would be the ones who discovered lodes of the ore in veins they were finding while digging on their claims.

The varied accounts concerning the exodus to that luring wonderland became the gist of many hair-raising accounts. And these accounts criss-crossed in reverberation along the mouth-to-mouth trails back east. The tales of those accounts trickling back to those common folks there in the Ohio settlement held great fascination, almost unbelief.

Like the stories told about the almost overnight "hey day" growth along what was called a new California "gold coast." Inevitably, along with the boom of new money, would be the boom of new business to satisfy the needs for celebration. This brought on the sudden building of hotels, the saloons with the whiskey, the girls, the glitter, the myriad of new business opportunities! The tales reaching back east were mind-boggling.

Although the bits of news about the changes and the happenings in those far off places were slow in reaching this eastern area, it was ever fresh to any ears hearing it for the first time. Often times, it was awesome and quite appalling.

That was the case in the late 1840s when the stories concerning a group called the "Donner party" began to circulate. Even the most obdurate became sickened.

These stories told about how that group had kept forging along on their destination to the far west. Unwisely they had kept on until it was too late in the season for traveling in that area. They became faced with severe wintry conditions there in the high altitude passageway in the forest-covered mountains of the eastern California territory. They found themselves stranded.

Those Donners, it was told, were caught there in that pass, completely isolated, helpless, and snowed-in for the following long winter months. The ones who did survive were not discovered until late springtime, when, finally, travelers could again forge through.

And it was then that bits of information about their tragedy began to surface back into the eastern part of the country.

That group of families had the snow to use for water, and that was life saving, but as their supplies had dwindled, their struggles had compounded. Their animals, the mules that had pulled their wagons, were killed, one by one, and their meat became nourishment. Accounts of sickness and exhaustion were being talked of, with mention of desperation that included cannibalism.

On the hearing of these heart-wrenching stories about such horrendous ordeals, the folks in Caleb Bennett's family were touched, especially Caleb and Minerva themselves. Just imagining the despair and the severity that went on in that mountainous camp struck a personal chord.

Although more than 40 years had elapsed since their own trek from Pennsylvania, some of the scars of their own hardships endured along that journey welled up in memory.

Although they'd had fewer miles to cover, and had started out in springtime, their own route had been unmarked and in places quite perilous. They themselves could attest to fear and loneliness.

These things being told now were also dredging up some memories about their feelings of homesickness for their families. About their missing the security of their old surroundings. Even though they'd been young with strong physical healthiness they remembered all that hard, backbreaking labor.

Caleb could picture that gaunt, weary little group found by the rescuers. A meal or two of good victuals would soon have them ready for travel, but it would take more than rich victuals to dull the horrors etched into the depths of their minds.

So now, with his younger ones spouting admonitions of what and whatnot they would have done had they been in that Donner party, like, *"well, I would have died first,"* Caleb could give them some wise thoughts for their minds to digest.

Caleb reckoned that until a person himself was faced with such a situation he was not qualified to make any kind of judgment. Caleb also reckoned that when faced with hungry little children, most likely, out of desperation, a person would resort to any available resource that was possible. And this was sobering and quieting.

Most of the talk by the people passing through, however, concerned tales of a more pleasant nature. A courier would wear an air of importance with his getting to tell about the many new changes that were constantly going on. In getting to elaborate on the growth that was taking place across the land.

And any listener in that Bennett settlement liked to be a participant in that kind of news. That kind of news was not so disturbing.

NINE

1850: A Winter Evening

Buttoning-up his coat, Ethan's eyes made one last swing of surveillance around the dimly lighted barn. Aware of that bitter cold waiting for him on just the other side of that barn door, for sure, once he got inside his warm house, he had no intention of having to come out any more tonight.

Satisfied that the animals were in good shape, he set about the final little task of extinguishing the lighted lanterns hanging from their hooks. Walking about the area, one by one, opening the little glass door in the side of each lantern globe, he blew out the flickering flame. Then, back at the barn door area, he slipped his hands into his warm gloves and carefully took down the last lighted lantern from its hook.

Tonight, it was his turn to close down the barn. The others had shared in getting the main chores done, like all the milking, and getting that milk attended to so each family would have its share. Then there'd been the feeding and the bedding-down of the animals. And, now, tonight, it was his job to be sure that each last little detail had been attended to.

Ethan and RoseMarie had their own house, while his two brothers with their families, his brother-in-law and sister, and his father and mother all lived in their own homes. The setting for each log house had been spaced and laid out there in the Bennett family glen.

From the beginning, as Caleb had watched each of his children grow, he'd begun his dream of their becoming adults and settling right there, forming a little family compound.

So, when the first son had married, Caleb's dream was put into operation. And, with the passing of a few years, happily biding his time, Caleb had lived the realization of his hopes.

That first house had been strategically set for access to the springhouse and water, to the barns, and to the little lumber mill by the river. And, of course, according to that mental plan in Caleb's dream, it had been set to allow the potential for a curving line that would be ready for further building!

With the many capable hands sharing all the responsibilities in the dealing with the daily livelihood, the chores were divided up. They were divided up agreeably and amiably. The same was family-handled concerning the work of the now very busy Bennett Lumber Mill. Life in the peaceful forest glen was good.

Now, bracing himself for that biting chill of the winter evening, Ethan opened the barn door and stepped out into the night. Routinely, he made certain the door was closed securely behind him. He felt confident he was leaving that barn area in ship-shape condition. And, in the darkness there before him, the soft glow of the lantern was marking the start of the snow-shoveled pathway leading to his own house.

At once, Ethan's spirit revved up. There ahead, 60 yards or so, was home, and the yellow lights showing from the windows were beckoning through the winter's early darkness.

This was the home that Ethan had built back in 1837 when he was getting ready to be married to RoseMarie. The home was built with logs and lumber from trees of the family forest that surrounded them still. And, built of course, with the help of his father and his older brothers.

No matter the season, Ethan always looked forward to this time of night. All the evening chores attended to, supper waiting and always smelling good, and always, his RoseMarie! Waiting for him, all full of loving smiles!

And the children. Even their noise was a welcoming music. Ah, those four children! They were Ethan's pride and joy.

There was his daughter, pretty Mary Rose, a copy of her mother. Turning 12, already she could handle just about any chore in the kitchen. And Tim, about 10 now, was becoming a regular hand. He was strong and dependable, both with his chores and in the family lumber mill. He'd begun helping there some, along with his older cousins.

Young John, the third child, was about 3 years behind his brother. John watched him, mimicking him, always wanting to help with the work, but all the time, it was quite obvious that he'd rather be playing.

And then, there was Carrie. Sweet little Carrie. She was becoming the family scholar. Even at age 6, she had begun keeping a little journal, recording happenings as observed through her childish eyes. From the time, almost, that she could hold a book she'd wanted to know what the words said.

RoseMarie had helped her, and little Carrie had been an avid learner, always inquisitive and methodical. She was showing a lot of the same traits as that of her Aunt Carrie. Her aunt, too, still liked to put events into words on paper, neatly and orderly, and young Carrie adored her.

Reaching the platform of the little stoop there at the kitchen doorway, Ethan stomped the snow from his heavy boots, then he opened the door and quickly stepped inside. He lost no time in getting that door closed again. Just entering had allowed a draft of cold winter to rush in with him!

Alerted by the stomping sounds, the children were ready for him. The two younger ones were talking at once. Tim came to take the lantern, blowing out the flame.

Ethan removed his gloves, and then his cap, laying them on the wooden shelf above the coat rack, a shelf already full with the children's winter gear. Unbuttoning his big coat, he hung it on one of the hooks below the shelf.

He was listening to those younger ones chatter, answering their queries, but all the while he was looking over their heads, across the room.

There by the kitchen stove stood his RoseMarie, wiping her hands on her apron, looking the picture of happiness. How Ethan reveled in this scene. As always, he could just feel the day's tiredness lifting from his whole being. What a blessing to relish!

He sat down then on the bench by the doorway. The remaining snow on his boots was beginning to melt in the warmth of the cheery room. As he started unlacing the strings of one high leather boot, Tim squatted down to unlace the other one.

What a picture! What contentment! Ethan loved these winter evenings. Stepping through the doorway into this family atmosphere, there was a transformation...instant and automatic. With his whole being swooped up in that loving peacefulness, any physical stress from his day's activity melted away like the snow on his boots.

"Supper's all ready, Ethan. And we'll give you just two minutes to wash up," RoseMarie called out, with that warm grin for him, and that aroma filling the room was verifying her message.

"I may need three minutes," Ethan responded, settling back a bit on the bench, still breathing in that whole panorama. But then he asked, "and just what is it that smells so good?"

Tim answered that one, "Rabbit and gravy! I went hunting this afternoon."

"And I baked the biscuits," chimed in Mary Rose.

"Well, then, I'd just better make this 2½ minutes." Ethan was getting to his feet as he spoke.

Striding over to the dry sink cabinet in his stocking feet, he began washing his hands and face. RoseMarie had the basin of water ready for him. The pretty flower decorated ewer, matching the basin, set there filled with water from the outside spring. But, she had already added some hot water from the stove's reservoir to the cold in the basin, knowing how good that would make Ethan feel.

The fire pot of the nearby kitchen range was kept filled with short lengths of split wood, burning with heat for the cooking and baking as well as keeping the water in the reservoir hot. Along with being the source for cooking, baking, and ready-hot water, that kitchen range also made a nice warm and cheery spot in the one-room log building.

There was a small loft above the room where the children slept, like in Caleb and Minerva's home, but all the family living was done in this one main room.

To keep that kitchen range fire going called for the chore of carrying in chopped, split wood. And the reservoir on the opposite end had to be kept filled with water. Also, carrying out the ashes from the firepot was among the daily chores.

The fireplace called for bigger logs, and those ashes had to be scooped up and carried outside also. But these chores were just a routine part of the lifestyle.

Drying his face, then his hands, Ethan was noting the goings-on of the finishing up of the supper table. Picking up the comb, he dipped it into the water in the washbasin, and then watching himself in the big mirror hanging above the washstand, he finished up his toiletry.

As he combed he could see his younger daughter's image reflecting in the mirror, and smiling, he remarked, "Carrie, you're getting to be a regular young lady, helping your mother and your sister like this. I'll bet they just couldn't get a meal without you," Ethan could just see his little girl's chest puff out.

Going to the table then, he pulled out the chair at his place, sitting down. The boys did as their father, sitting at their regular places. Young Carrie, setting the plate of hot biscuits in front of her father, looked smugly satisfied.

Everyone in his place, unfolding his napkin and laying it across his lap, each bowed his head and waited quietly. The meal began after Ethan said a few words of thanks for the food before them and for their many blessings.

"Well, now, let's see just how this rabbit of Tim's tastes," Ethan commented as he forked a piece of the fried meat. Taking a bite of that biscuit with the hot rabbit gravy dripping from it, he said, "M-mm, this is so good!"

Savoring a couple more mouthfuls of the food, he said, "Do you know what? I was just thinking…if we had some of those tender green fiddleheads from the ferns along with some of those fresh mushrooms from the woods. They'd be all hot and buttered like your mother cooks them. Wouldn't they go good along with this? We'd really be a family of royals, now wouldn't we!"

But Tim said," Well, it's a long time 'til spring, Father."

Amid the eating, and the family conversations, Ethan asked, "Tim, did you get your gun cleaned and oiled when you came in with it?" To which young Tim replied, "Yes, sir, I always take care of that." Ethan expected that answer. He had taught each of his young sons well in the care of a gun. How to respect it, and how keeping it clean and ready was an important requisite.

As a fact, in the family life of any settler, firearms were a necessary part of survival, both in putting meat on the table as well as for safety from the wild animals that were known to be in the area.

Even the domestic animals, like pigs and beef, were most often shot for butchering. And the meat for many a meal was from the deer or the wild turkeys that roamed the woods and were so plentiful throughout the year.

The supper ended with a blackberry cobbler. RoseMarie had made it, using a home-canned jar of berries picked and canned the past summer.

As part of the supper preparation, Mary Rose had dipped up generous portions putting them into the six dessert bowls. Little Carrie had then set a filled bowl at each place setting. It was a pleasurable part of the meal, now and then, to eye and anticipate the finishing off of that bowl of satisfying deliciousness.

At the right moment, when each dinner plate was looking empty, and that dessert bowl was placed on it, the pitcher of cream was passed around. And then that "finishing off" began!

When the meal was over, Ethan tended to the fires. First in the kitchen range, using some smaller pieces of split wood. Then, he re-stoked the fireplace, laying on some bigger logs from the supply stack.

As usual, the boys had done their evening chores well. They had carried in the bigger wood along with the smaller split wood, neatly stacking it in back of the kitchen range. Also, they'd filled the bushel basket with kindling, all ready for starting a fire in the morning.

Too, the boys had refilled all the fresh water containers, carrying them in from the spring.

Now, with the fires burning cheerily, Ethan got settled comfortably in his black horsehide leather chair, resting his feet on the little handmade wooden footstool. He gave an audible sigh of complete contentment, thinking, *"Ah, what a way to end up a day!"*

RoseMarie seemingly gliding about the kitchen area, was finishing up from supper with the help of the girls.

Young John was sitting, cross-legged, on the homemade crocheted rug on the floor by the fireplace. His nimble fingers were wielding a big-sized, hand-whittled wooden crochet hook. He was working meticulously on turning out a little oval shaped "throw rug" identical to the bigger one on which he was sitting.

He was crocheting from a ball made of a one-inch wide, continuous strip of cloth. The strip had been cut from odds and ends of cotton materials. During free times, RoseMarie or one of the girls had cut the strips of whatever lengths from whatever handy pieces of cloth that became available. Some were from worn out garments that still had some good patches of cloth. Then, again during free times, they had hand-sewn these shorter piece lengths into one long continuous strip, winding it onto the big ball.

Now, using the wooden hook, John was crocheting, adeptly, having been well taught by his mother.

Tim, also quite adeptly and well taught by his father or his uncles, was whittling.

Sitting on a kitchen chair and holding over a bucket for catching the shavings, he was whittling away at hollowing out a rectangular piece of wood. He was envisioning a finished lidded wooden box. He was making it for his mother for holding some of her little keepsakes.

As he whittled away, knowing he'd be needing many such winter evenings for completion, he kept thinking about a design he might choose for carvings on the exterior of the box.

The more Tim whittled, the better adept he was becoming. As Ethan watched him, sensing the pride and love the boy was putting into the work, he was thinking, *"that truly will be a treasure box!"*

Taking all this in, Ethan was a happy man, especially so, as he watched his RoseMarie. His heart would fairly burst with his love for her. He just never could get enough of watching her. He sensed her happiness. It generated from her as she fairly flitted about, tending to her many tasks, all the while questioning the children, or answering their queries to her. She never failed to stir urges within him to accomplish bigger things. With her beside him, always he felt impelled to strive toward doing just that. And it was at these times the loving bond between them was further nurtured.... further strengthened.

From the day they'd married, back there in 1837, when she'd become his bride at a community "gathering" with all the other families beaming joyously as they looked on, he could barely contain all his love and his pride.

Sitting there now, quietly, Ethan continued to watch each busy family member. Now and then there was a crackling of the burning flames as the fire was drawing up the chimney. This added to the cheery homeness. His thoughts began to ramble.

He was deciding, with many such wintry nights ahead 'til springtime, he needed another project of his own to be working at. And watching RoseMarie as she went about her kitchen work, he knew just what that project ought to be!

He could see that she needed a small worktable there in that kitchen area, and his mind began to picture it. He remembered, at the Trading Post, he'd seen some white porcelain casters. Each caster had a metal-banded framework that would give it durability. With them on the legs of a table, she could roll it around wherever she needed it. He just knew it would be a welcomed help to her. And he knew she would appreciate it.

Straightening up in his chair, he said, "Tim, tomorrow you and I are going tree hunting. I'm going to make your mother a new worktable.

Tim's ears perked up. And RoseMarie became all excited and full of questions.

TEN

A Table of Oak

As usual with the dawn the Bennett family complex came awake.

Lights from the kerosene lamps began to appear, dimly showing out the windows of each of the log homes. Roosters began to crow. Then, lantern lights began to show at the barn.

The atmosphere reverberated with a familiar blend of sounds from the animals. A new day was beginning in that Bennett glen, nestled there in the forest by the Ohio River.

It was later in the morning when Ethan managed the time to gather his young son, Tim, his axes, a sturdy log chain, his saws, laying all the gear on the skid. The skid was hitched up to the double tree of the team's harness. And the two of them, the father and the son, left the mill area, heading out into the woods.

Back in that era, back there in 1850, it was mostly through his father's teaching and his own personal physical experience that Ethan had become knowledgeable concerning trees and wood.

On this morning he was looking for just the right oak to make RoseMarie's table. And he knew he would be picking a white oak. The wood of a white oak always got prettier as it aged, and he wanted RoseMarie's table to be special.

Already familiar with a certain group of just such trees, he drove the horses as closely as he could there in the forest, to that area. They walked about, eyeing the various choices. "Here it is, Tim. This one is it. It'll make a beautiful table! You just wait and see." Ethan was excited. He was anxious to get started.

Ten-year-old Tim was ready. He loved working with his father. And his young muscles, already husky and sturdy from his part in the daily existence, would keep up his end on that crosscut saw.

Once the big tree was felled, they further sawed it into lengths that they could handle. Then the logs were dragged to where they could be loaded onto the big hand-built skid. One by one, they would wrap the log chain around a log, and then attach the big iron hook on the other end of the chain to the harness of the team. Then the horses dragged the log through the trees to the more open space where the skid was waiting.

In this wintry time of year, with the foliage brown and dry, trimming off the redundant branches was easy. The usable smaller branches would be hauled back to the mill to make trimming boards or maybe they would be used for firewood.

With such a big tree, several trips of skid loads would have to be made to get all the pieces of the wood dragged back to the mill.

For this trip, Ethan and Tim left with a choice larger log, with some of the smaller cuts chained around it. With needing to get back to help with the routine evening chore time, the other logs were left there in the little clearing. They'd be waiting to be handled as time allowed.

Also, as time allowed, Ethan turned that choice log into lumber. The procedures were laborious, in spite of Caleb's keeping up by adding a steam-powered engine for running the saw. Ethan was ever thankful in appreciation of the progressive strides his father had made. When building those first log houses, there had been no such thing as the mill. Ethan's siblings each shared in that thankfulness as well.

Once the boards were made, Ethan measured, and by hand he sawed the smaller cuts that he would be needing. He had the design for the table all figured out in his mind. Then once he had these smaller pieces ready, he had carried them into the house.

Now, during the evenings there with his family in his own little cheery wintry haven, he had his own little project with which to keep busy.

Meticulously he worked to fit those pieces together. He was so very careful to match up the grain of the boards that he'd chosen for the tabletop. Carefully he smoothed the wood using a handheld plane, then with an emery stone, he worked painstakingly to make it splinter free and smooth.

The casters, the pretty ones of white porcelain, were implanted last, one into each leg.

Then came the final procedure. Ethan could foresee the portable table becoming a big helpmate to RoseMarie in her kitchen work. He wanted to coat it with a protective covering that would protect the finish, but also allow the oaken grain to beautify as it aged. Tung oil seemed to be the best he had to use for this.

With his fingers he rubbed that tung oil over the entire table surface, using a piece of rag to wipe off any excess. Then, over a several evening period, Ethan repeated these applications with lots of hand rubbing for smoothness. And each coat would dry during the daytime. The wood responded to the gentle smoothing with a beautiful shine.

On one evening as springtime was nearing, Ethan was ready. His finished project satisfied him. With a bit of fun "todo" fanfare, not to mention his pride, he presented RoseMarie with that welcomed piece of kitchen furniture.

With its shiny smooth top, so well supported by those four legs that Ethan so painstakingly had decorated with his own hand carvings, it was reflecting the many hours of loving labor he'd put into it during those family winter evenings.

Also reflecting was the love and excitement on Ethan's pretty wife's face. During those evenings, as her own hands had been busy with mending or knitting, when she'd seen Ethan attach those fancy white porcelain casters, then roll the table back and forth testing them, she'd already begun anticipating her usage of it. She could see how it was going to shorten her lifting and carrying.

Now, she just knew it was going to be so hard to wait for morning. She was so anxious to begin rolling that new table around in her little workspace preparing breakfast.

Yes, RoseMarie knew. Her tomorrow was going to be a special day!

ELEVEN

Scars from the Civil War

Those years of the 1850s were fast changing times. Not only was the business of the Bennett lumber mill steadily expanding, but also life itself had taken on an expanded outlook.

More and more, with the passing of each year, the attentions of the families in that settlement were no longer confined just to matters of personal daily livelihood. That had become easier with the aid of new products and new easier methods in work habits. With this easing, along with improvements in communication with outside affairs, there had come a feeling of belonging to and being a part of this bigger world.

There continued to be news exchanged and discussed about growth and changes throughout the land, but now this was being interspersed with the nation's political concerns. Political views and prevalent opinions of the leaders of the various states had become serious subjects.

There was one man in particular who was looming in importance throughout these political views. This was a man named Abraham Lincoln.

In learning about Mr. Lincoln's background, the Bennett family had become quite impressed. Hearing about his early meager childhood, they could relate personally to such stories. And they'd always felt that such a beginning had a way of building strength in character.

In their reading of accounts about Mr. Lincoln and in talking with others, they had learned about his being born in a small log cabin setting at the top of a hill in a little farming area of Hodgenville, Kentucky. That had been in 1809. It was said that young Abraham, when just a small boy, had been taught how to read and to write by his mother. They would do this, sitting by the light of the fireplace in their one little room log home.

Then in 1816 the Lincoln family had left Kentucky, going over to the Sprinklesburg and Boonville area in the new Warrick County in Indiana. When he was only 8 years old his mother died, and she was buried in that Indiana locality. But very soon after, in 1819, his father married again and the young Abraham had bonded well with this new stepmother.

It was said that young Abraham was always interested in the field of law. While living in that Indiana area he frequently walked to Boonville to borrow books from the Boonville attorney, John Brackenridge. And whenever he knew his friend was to plead a case, Abraham would go there to the courthouse to listen and to learn.

As a young man, Mr. Lincoln, striking out on his own, had engaged in many things, but always still studied law books with diligence. He had gone to Illinois, and in 1831 he had hired on to take cargo down the Mississippi River to New Orleans. This was done on a flatboat.

Coming back to Illinois he settled for a time in New Salem, a town of about 100 people, along the Sangamon River. Here he engaged in many jobs. For a time he was a clerk in a general store.

And it was said that, along with others he had helped in driving animals to market along a wagon road there in Illinois. This dirt road began at the Ohio River at the south of the state and ended miles north at the big busy market in Chicago. And along this well-marked trail, cattle, goats, swine, even flocks of turkeys and chickens, were herded north on treks to the big market.

Now, as Mr. Lincoln was becoming popular, this road was claiming fame and it was becoming known as the "Lincoln Trail."

But, all this while, Abraham was reading about and studying law, determined on becoming a lawyer. In 1836 Mr. Lincoln was admitted to the bar realizing that goal he had set for himself. By then he had settled in Springfield, the capitol of Illinois.

In 1842, there in Springfield, he had married a lady called Mary Todd. She was the daughter of a well-known Kentucky banker and quite an accomplished socialite.

Nearing the ending of the 1850's decade, the country had filled with unrest. The subject of slavery in the southern states was leading toward a division between those states and the states of the north.

Throughout this troubled period, Abraham Lincoln was steadily gaining a stronger popularity. Although he himself had been born in the slave state of Kentucky, he deeply opposed slavery. But his strongest belief was that the north and the south could never survive unless they were a united nation.

During these years with his being actively engaged in political affairs, he was building a trust and a confidence throughout the northern states. This was especially true amongst the common people. During those early years of growing into manhood and dealing with many people while working at varied trades, he had earned the reputation of being a most honest fellow.

Folks remembered him as being a most intelligent and sensible man. Then, through his work as a lawyer, traveling for days at a time to communities where cases were being tried, these qualities were continuously surfacing. Mr. Lincoln was fast impressing many folks. And he was more and more taking part in these civil affairs.

Throughout these stressful times, Ethan Bennett along with his brothers and other family men were working long hours operating the mill. They were filling government orders for lumber as well as taking care of their regular customers.

Caleb was at the mill every day along with the others, but he was beginning to feel some limitations due to all his years of hard physical work. Wisely, now he was playing the role of supervising and letting his sons take over more and more of the heavier load.

Seemingly, things were running along smoothly. But that foreboding gloom of unrest that hovered over the country was reaching into the family glen as well.

With the threat of secession of some of the southern states, the eminent likelihood of an actual war was having to be faced. This was most discerning to those Bennett fathers. They didn't often speak of it aloud in words, but each felt a heaviness within his heart.

Ethan's son, Timothy, was married now. And while the boy would be needed in the mill in producing the extra lumber that was sure to be a requisite in the event of war, he might rather volunteer for duty.

Mary Rose, too, was married. And her strong and healthy young husband would have those same options as Tim.

Then, there was young John…18 years old and prime for soldiering!

Ethan handled these troubling thoughts by delving deeper and harder into his work. That helped some in not allowing the time to study about it.

And RoseMarie was wearing her concern on her face.

Young Carrie was a worry of a different sort. She was enrolled in the Delaney Academy over west in Newburgh, Indiana, Major Sprinkle's old Sprinklesburg. She was doing quite well, learning to be a schoolteacher, and loving it, both the schooling and the family with which she was boarding. But these days, for her parents, well, she was just too far away from home.

1860 came and Abraham Lincoln was nominated for the presidency of the United States. His political activity had gained him renown, and many of his quotes made from time to time were being touted and repeated. Like his declaring at his party's State Convention "a state divided against itself cannot stand." And Mr. Lincoln was predicting the eventual triumph of freedom.

All this led to Mr. Lincoln being voted in as president of the United States. Meaning, he was voted into being the leader of a nation that was splitting in turmoil and bitterness.

On March 4, 1861, he was inaugurated into office as president. But seven southern states, South Carolina, Mississippi, Florida, Alabama, Georgia, Louisiana and Texas, had adopted ordinances of secession. And the Confederate States of America was formed with Jefferson Davis as its president.

In his inaugural address, President Lincoln held that secession was illegal and stated that he intended to maintain federal possessions in the South.

Soon after, on April 12, when an attempt was made to resupply Fort Sumter, a federal installation at Charleston, South Carolina, the Southern artillery opened fire.

Three days later President Lincoln called for troops to put down the rebellion. In response, Virginia, Arkansas, North Carolina and Tennessee joined the Confederacy.

And…a civil war between the states had begun!

Neither side was prepared for war, but it began with each side confident that there would be an early victory!

Young John Bennett, all his 18 years of gentle compassion at once becoming patriotically vibrant, couldn't wait to answer his country's call for troops.

Of course Ethan and RoseMarie were proud of their son, but it was with aching hearts that they held him closely, bidding him goodbye as he was leaving home for duty.

With his little area being totally militarily unorganized, John headed east to the Cincinnati port area where a command post was operating. There he was sworn in as an infantryman in the Union Army and he was given his uniform.

Again with the yet unorganized chaotic system prevailing, John's orders, along with a few other new young enlistees, were to report for duty at the headquarters in Newburgh, Indiana.

John was disappointed. He had envisioned an arena with some action. While his very nature was averse to discord, always liking an environment of harmony, he was appalled by the thought of any human soul being abased to the level of slavehood. And he was ready to fight hard for every person's right to be free as an individual.

With Newburgh's rapid growth and development, and becoming such a renowned and busy river port, it did hold a fascination for young John. The area was such a contrast to his small Trading Post and settlement area. Then too, his sister Carrie would be nearby at the Academy.

So John settled in, dutifully bent on becoming a good soldier.

His aptitude for neat, thorough clerical work gained his superiors' attention and appreciation, and early on, John was well on his way to becoming a reliable and valuable war aide.

With only the river separating those army headquarters from the enslaved state of Kentucky, Newburgh became a well-stocked garrison of ammunition. And its hospital was kept busy with caring for wounded soldiers brought in from battles waged elsewhere.

A bit over a year into the war had gone by when Newburgh found itself involved in a one-sided skirmish.

It was now July of 1862, and on the 17th, through a strategically well-planned ruse, a surprise raid was successfully carried out on those Newburgh headquarters by a Confederate general, Adam Johnson.

Quietly and unobserved in the darkness of night, this Confederate Brig. Gen. Adam Johnson with his little band of thirty-two guerrilla soldiers, managed to cross the Ohio River from the opposite Kentucky shore. Then, in complete surprise, they took command of the Newburgh operation.

Gen. Johnson had appeared quite ominous and powerful as he announced that a large garrison was just across on the Kentucky side of the river, just waiting for the order to attack. And this was most believable.

The Union soldiers could look across to see what appeared to be a large cannon set up over there on that opposite shore. The cannon was aimed in their direction and they could make out Confederate sentry men marching back and forth with their horses, in readiness. With no resistance, Johnson and his men looted and ransacked the town and the Union hospital.

Johnson didn't make prisoners of the eighty or so wounded Union soldiers, but he made them swear that they would never again take up arms against the Confederacy. Even some Confederacy sympathizers there in Newburgh aided those Confederate men, helping them to get back safely across the river.

When morning and daylight came, on July 18th, 1862, when all the confusion had been sorted through and order had again settled in, the real truth became known.

Cleverly, Gen. Johnson had set up that little stage. His men had tied two lengths of ordinary stovepipe to a smooth black-charred log, arranging a pipe on either side. Then they had mounted their creation onto a wagon, aiming it toward the Union garrison across the river.

With his sentry men posted, marching back and forth, guarding it, under the shroud of darkness, the set-up of a large garrison had seemed very real and very ominous.

It was inevitable that Newburgh, henceforth, would have the reputation of being the site of the first known Confederate raid north of the Mason-Dixon line, with that raid having occurred without a single shot being fired.

Even so, the community of Newburgh's thankfulness that it had not experienced death and destruction during that raid more than compensated for any chiding it had to live down.

Many were the hard and bitter battles waged during the next years that followed. Battles that took sad and heavy tolls on both sides. Heavy tolls in lives that were lost, in soldiers that were wounded, and in the utter devastation and destruction.

It was in 1865, when President Lincoln declared Ulysses S. Grant as commander-in-chief over the entire Union army, that the war became more favorable for the Union Side.

And it was in early April of that year, during the battle at Appomattox, when Gen. Robert E. Lee surrendered to Gen. Grant. This took place at the Courthouse there in southwestern Virginia. With that, the remaining Confederate armies quickly collapsed, and at long last, the Civil War ended.

At long last young John Bennett prepared to go home.

It had been his option to take the stagecoach for making his trip home. Although it would take a few more days, John looked forward to being out in the country again. Finally away from duty, he felt he needed an interlude with some undemanding personal time.

The war had been long and hard. John had been forced to grow up. He knew things were never going to be the same again. Not ever. And now he wanted to just whoa down a moment and do some sorting out. He knew there were going to be adjustments to face the moment he stepped out of that uniform and getting back into his regular clothes.

It was going to be so good to get out of this uniform but he wondered if his old clothes would still fit. He felt sure, though, that his mother had kept them.

Riding along in the stage, John smiled, thinking about all these things. He thought about his family and his actually getting to be with them again after such a long, long time.

Emotions began to stir up inside him, emotions that John had been forced to keep depressed for too long.

Now, as he and his two fellow travelers jostled along, John checked his pocket watch. It was 3:15 in the afternoon. That meant there were still a few more hours to go before they were due to reach the next Trading Post where they'd be spending the night.

John was looking forward to that Trading Post, to get out of these confining coach quarters and to move around and to stretch. Dinner at a table would be good too. The contents of the small-boxed lunch packed by that morning's Post were beginning to wear thin. Time was going slowly even with the 4-horse hitch pulling the coach along at a good steady trot.

John settled back against the softness of the leather upholstery, closing his eyes. His fellow travelers were doing the same.

The rhythmic din of the muted voices of the driver and his stagehand blending in with the clopping of the horses' hoofs with the rolling along of the wheels wafted into the small enclosure. John liked those two men out there on the driver's seat. He'd gotten to know a bit about them during these last days.

Dakota Bear, the driver called himself! Not liking the severity of the northern territory winters, he said he'd come a bit south when those states were becoming more settled and organized. With stagecoach routes becoming regulated, he'd become a regular driver. With his husky build, his bushy hair and beard, he fit his name. And with his carefree and friendly nature, he was most likable. John felt that he was dependable and trustworthy.

It took a man of muscle to lug around the harness and to handle the reins of a hitch in all the situations confronted along the routes. The horses were often spooked in a storm or frightened by the sudden appearance of an animal. And some weather conditions would call for some manual digging out. Or a broken coach wheel could require some lifting. Dakota Bear had adapted well to his role.

Nate, his helper, with his shotgun always within easy reach, was a good aide, not only with the teams but helping in tending to the needs of the fares as well.

With each mile now, home was beginning to feel closer to John. He had noted that even the terrain was beginning to look a bit familiar to him. They'd left the flatter land of Indiana as the road had veered more to the north. Heading northeasterly, they were moving away from the Ohio River where for miles it had been dipping up and down, forming the state line that marked off Kentucky.

Now their road was heading toward that southwestern corner of Ohio where the river would be flowing from the north.

Now the land was more rolling and the road was winding in and out along the lowlands, dodging those hills. Another night out and they should be just about reaching that Ohio corner. Then, not too many miles beyond, all nestled there amidst the surrounding forest, would be home. Home, with that little familiar settlement of the families he knew, and then John's beloved Bennett glen.

During those past years, involved with the terrors of the war, John, through duty, had been forced to embody a strict disciplined military routine. Good soldiering operates from the basis of sound judgment with sentiment laid aside. This tends to emit a coldness that a true soldier must acquire. And John had strived to be a good military man.

Even though his Newburgh headquarters were too small to be considered a Confederacy threat, he had confronted that military environment at such a young age. Too often his days were grim with his paper work requiring face-to-face contact of the wounded coming into the hospital.

Through them he had witnessed the reality of the battlefield aftermath. He knew the heart-wrenching stories of too many of those men.

Some of those soldiers could be patched up and returned to battle. But too often they were beyond repair. Many were tragic cases where the physical wounds were complicated by ones indelibly etched into their minds. These were of a deeper damage, and that little Union hospital had no effective treatment for them.

Riding along now his body stiffened in recalling these thoughts. Would he ever again be able to free his mind of the repulsiveness of the experiences of those war years? Would he ever again know those light-hearted and carefree feelings of those days before enlisting?

On an impulse John reached for his personal gear bag laying there at his side. He pulled out a small ledger booklet; picking up a pencil packed there along side the book. Thumbing through to a blank page, his pencil ready, he sat quietly for a time, thinking and remembering. Then he began to write.

"May, 1865. As I near the close of this long journey, I can smile and say that even the dust from the road smells good. This is my journey that will separate the horrors of those war years, miles back there behind me, from the specialness of home and family laying just ahead. The only thing I want to bring from those years back there behind me is that image I was able to concoct and embrace during the darkness of those nights. After the hard trials of the day, that image would sustain me. I'd lie there on my cot and I'd pretend that I was that young boy again at home. I'd be in our forest glen. Sometimes it was snowy winter, and I'd be sitting on the rug by the fireplace, one of the rugs I'd made from one of those balls of rags. Sometimes it was summery, and I could hear the hoot of an owl, or a raccoon as it foraged for something to eat. Sensing that protective shield of the woods around me, I would feel safe. I'd feel all wrapped-up in the love of our family. And, lying there, within that image, I'd feel so warm and safe. I would relax and go to…"

Abruptly, outside, bedlam erupted!

There was shouting in the air. There was a commotion of horses other than that of the hitch. Dakota Bear was hollering "Whoa," to the hitch. The coach zigzagged and twisted to a stop. Startled, those three passengers bolted to an upright attention.

A deep male voice was commanding, "Git yer hands up 'n keep 'em up. You, there, with that shotgun…jest hand it over, nice 'n easy. Git it, Hank…we got' im covered."

Amid the commotion, then, John heard that deep voice that seemed to be in charge holler out, "Now, don't ya try no funny stuff. We'uns don't aim ta hurt ya! Hank, you git ther stuff up thar off the top. Git ther wallets. An,' Sonny, you tend ta the ones inside." And the coach door was jerked open.

There stood a young man that had to be just a kid. But his hand looked menacing holding a gun pointed at those three inside. A riding horse with the reins hanging loosely waited just behind him. A dirty looking rag covered the lower half of his face. His tousled, unkempt brownish hair was straggling from under his dirty looking black hat.

"Git out here, wher' I kin see ya," the young man ordered. And, with the gun pointed directly at John, he moved back a bit, making room, saying, "You first, git out here with yer hands up."

Trying to keep his hands held up, yet needing to clutch the stage hand-holds for balance, John made it out and stood there before the young marauder. The other two passengers followed quietly, their hands held high as well.

At a glance, sizing up the situation, John could see his group's vulnerability. It had all happened so suddenly there had been no time to prepare. And with their advantage by the surprise element, the marauders meant to lose no time. John noted they were in a bend of the road with a patch of trees growing on either side.

Besides the kid, there were three more of them. Older men, with two of them remaining on their horses, their guns trained on Dakota Bear and Nate who were still sitting on the stagecoach seat. The third one was dismounted, very busy at gathering up any loot available. Each lower face was covered with a piece of soiled looking cloth, and each was armed with a gun belt showing pistols in addition to their rifles.

John knew their only chance was to keep quiet and obey any orders.

Standing there, in his blue Union soldier uniform, complete with the medals he'd earned during his war duties, John was a good head taller than the young man with the gun.

"Damn it, Sonny, don't jest stand thar. We got our guns on all of 'em. Git ther stuff!" barked out that older voice.

But Sonny, confronted by that uniform, was losing his boldness. With his free hand he'd begun to pull at the rag across his nose and cheeks as if suddenly he wasn't getting enough air. John looked so authoritative standing there, so straight, so orderly. He looked so big. He appeared threatening and dangerous.

But, again came that demanding voice, "Damn it, Sonny, do yer job, ya damn know-nuthin' kid!"

With eyes looking straight at John, gesturing with his gun, but with his hand clearly trembling, Sonny yelled out, "Aw right, all 'a ya, take ever'thing out 'a yer pockets. Ease 'em down on the ground."

Now, during that next moment it was never clear about just what took place.

When John lowered his hands, moving to take out his pocket watch, a shot resounded, piercing that tense air.

And in the fleeting of one brief, idiotic moment, two young lives were forever changed. An instant change that clearly reflected from those two faces.

John went limp. All those fresh dreams and that boyish tenderness ever coursing through that caring heart were lifted to a higher level. And as the tangible residue of his body's empowerment was fast staining the ground where he fell, John's countenance became soft and gentle.

That other young face showed a moment of terror. Then it whitened, and the young hand holding the gun went limp, sagging down to the side. The other hand was jerking away the rag. On that face, an etching of steeliness set in. It was a look of hard steeliness that only would deepen with time.

Like a rude trespasser, that rough commanding voice cut through that solemn silence, "Well, suh-un-of-uh-bitch, Sonny, yah sure messed things up now! Well, git ther stuff, 'n let's git out 'a here. Ya damn greenhorn, know-nuthin' kid."

And that young boy…he couldn't have been more than fifteen…began to gather what loot he could find. And with that rifle trained on them, those sickened passengers just let it happen.

With the passengers' luggage bags tied and thrown across the horses along with their own saddle bags holding wallets, rings and watches, plus balancing the guns while holding the reins, the marauders rode off into the grove of trees and disappeared.

And, just for an instant, the four men that were left there, big burly Dakota Bear and Nate, sitting on their seat, and the two passengers standing by the open door of the stage, remained motionless in disbelieving shock.

Such a gruesome circumstance there in that little bend in the road in that lonely isolated countryside in the middle of the afternoon.

But the blowing and the snorting of the horses, the stomping of a hoof and the jangling of the harness as a head tossed up and down or a tail switched back and forth fending off flies, brought the starkness of the reality. There was a grim and heart-wrenching task awaiting. The only thing they could do was get on with the trip.

Dakota Bear and Nate spread out a tarp. Then, with the help of the two passengers, they laid John's body on it, wrapping it carefully. With the hot sun shining down on the now empty luggage area of the coach roof, there was no other option but to transport John on one of the seats inside.

Gingerly, talking only as necessary, they arranged that tarp-wrapped bulk as best they could to make it fit on the narrow seat. Anticipating the jolting on the ride ahead, they used a rope for anchoring.

It was a saddened four-man cortege that set out to complete those last several hours to the next Trading Post. And the delay forced the last of those miles to be traveled through black darkness. Dakota Bear appreciated his hitch, entrusting the horses' instinct to follow the roadway.

Once they reached the Trading Post, amid the flurry of relating explanations of why they'd been overdue, there was help in getting things squared away.

The local man who served as a mortician took charge of John's body. And a young man volunteered to ride to the next Post, and then on to the Bennetts to inform them of their son. He said he would wait 'til early morning daylight to begin that trip. It was then that Dakota Bear brought out John's ledger. He handed it to that young man. And the young man promised that he would make sure that John's family got it.

The ledger had been left laying on the floor of the stage, appearing unimportant. But Dakota Bear had picked it up, knowing how very important it would be to John's family.

TWELVE

A Time for Adjustment

Pushing his chair back from the table, Ethan stood up, and folding his napkin still in his hand he placed it alongside his empty supper plate. Then he took the couple of steps to RoseMarie's chair, bent down to her giving her an affectionate kiss on the cheek. Straightening up, smiling, he said, "There, my kiss for the cook for such a good meal."

Going then to his daughter-in-law, Tim's Martha, with a bit of ado he kissed her lightly on her cheek as well, adding, "And one for this other fine cook!" Looking then toward his son, he added, "Tim, aren't we a couple of lucky men? Not only do we have these great cooks but we've got ourselves two pretty girls as well!"

Martha squeezed his arm, saying, "No, Ethan, we women are the lucky ones and we both know it!"

Going over to the fireplace then, using the poker, Ethan stirred up the fire, adding some more logs. Then he got all settled in his big chair. For a moment, he just sat there, breathing in the warmth of all this family specialness.

He listened to the women as they busied themselves with the kitchen clean-up chores. Martha was stopping now and then to tend to some need of her little three-year-old Ruth. And he was hearing young Timmy, the five-year-old, busy at play sitting on the oval rug in front of the fireplace. Little Timmy's dad, big Tim, was telling him about the time when he was a little guy like Timmy, riding horseback. He hadn't ducked low enough when passing under a limb of a tree. Yanked off backward from the horse, he had landed on the ground.

Amid Timmy's laughter, his dad showed the scar the limb had left under his chin.

How Ethan loved these evenings.

Tim and his Martha lived there with Ethan and RoseMarie, and those two young tykes kept the household livened up.

When Tim and Martha had married, it had seemed best for them to live with the older folks. John was off at War and Carrie was at the Delaney Academy in Newburgh, Indiana, training to be a teacher. In spite of the heavy workload at the family mill, Ethan and Tim had managed to get a room added on to the back of the main log house.

In putting on that room they had applied some of the newer technology. Using sawed lumber for the main structure, they had sided it with clapboards made of wood.

Ethan sat there, smiling contentedly. A day's work finished, a good supper and an easy chair were refreshing his tired body. But, as he watched the two Tims, busy there in front of the open fire, an aching pang of bitter-sweetness flashed through Ethan. It was at times like just now, with his seeing little Timmy sitting there on that crocheted rag rug on the floor, just like John used to do, that the awful void from John's absence reared up in painful reality.

Ethan's mind began mulling over the many family changes that had taken place during those war years.

Mary Rose and her little family lived nearby, and they were doing well in making their adjustments following her Frank's discharge from duty. He'd come home with only one hand. He had been all weakened and worn out following his close call with having to fight infection.

Carrie was teaching school up in the settlement. She was boarding with one of the families there, and she stayed busy with her work. She did get home now and then on the weekends.

It was almost April now, and it was beginning to feel like spring. Come May, a whole year would have passed since that day when that young man had ridden in to bring word of John and that horrible tragedy.

A whole year since Ethan and RoseMarie had been faced with devastation they'd never before known. Never before had anything so dear and personal been taken away from them. But, they'd picked up with life. And work had to go on. The others of the family were important as well. So he and his RoseMarie had learned to keep their ache, for the most part, on the inside.

Still, like at this moment, with seeing little Timmy there on the rug, it triggered a flash of memory that Ethan had to handle. Instantly surfacing came those feelings of things following that dreadful day last year, in 1865, when the young courier had ridden in with that awful message.

He was reminded of that return trip home from that Trading Post, driving the wagon and coming down their roadway leading into the Bennett glen. It was a remembrance well seared into Ethan's mind.

On that wagon seat with him had been his son Timothy. And riding along too was his aging father. Caleb had insisted that he had to go on that mission as well. In the back of that wagon had been the long wooden burial box. They were toting John home to lay him to rest in the little hallowed spot there in the family glen.

Ethan was remembering how all during that long, bitter war, when the nightfall of each day was ending without a courier having come with any dreaded news, then, for one more day, he and RoseMarie could breathe their thankfulness.

Then, finally, when the news had come of the war's end, their humble blessedness had been so deeply felt. At long last they could feel assured that John was safe and that he would be returning back home unharmed.

They'd begun to think about some celebrating for his homecoming. Their smiles, at last, were brighter. But then had come that courier.

Ethan had fashioned a marker, building it out of wood. Painstakingly, Tim, the carver, had inscribed the words, "John Caleb Bennett – May 12, 1865 – Age 22." Tenderly they'd laid John to rest but the hurts and the sadness didn't get buried in that grave, nor were they exposed on that marker.

Gradually, though, with the passing of each day blending in along with the routine of life, the aches could be pushed down, to the inside, making them a little easier to tolerate.

But, throughout all the land that was holding the ashes of that long and bitter war, there was too much tell tale evidence protruding from amongst those ashes. Ashes of this kind could not be just carried out for the wind to lightly blow away. Not with all that ever present evidence such as missing limbs, and the other ugly scars from battle wounds. Especially when meeting the eyes that failed to veil the broken hearts.

RoseMarie and Ethan, though, had decided that it would only magnify John's loss if they allowed all the happy life as he had known and loved to wither and die with him. And mixing good memories in with the hard ones had a way of wrapping up his sacrifice with even more honor and reverence.

Sitting there now, these thoughts flashing through his mind, involuntarily Ethan gave an audible sigh.

RoseMarie was just coming back from throwing the pan of dishwater out across the grass at the side of the kitchen door. Wiping the inside of the pan dry, smiling and looking toward him, she said, "Well, Ethan, what brought that on? Are you tired?"

"No, not now," he answered. "Watching all of you, and feeling and hearing the fire as it burns always takes the tiredness right out of me."

"Well, Martha and I are just about done here. I'm soon gonna join you and I'll see for myself it that's true," and she rolled her little worktable over to the kitchen cupboard. The little table was holding the clean and dried supper dishes, and now they were ready to be put away.

Now and then the fire would make a crackling noise as the flames flickered about the logs and Ethan watched the sparks draw toward the chimney.

His mind, now, was turning to some other thoughts he'd been considering lately and he was thinking it was about time that he should be sharing these thoughts with RoseMarie. In fact he was anxious to make known the plan to her that he'd been conceiving in his mind.

Tim's Martha gathered up her sewing basket. She got all settled in her rocker and began stitching on the gingham dress she was making for little Ruth. She was working on the hem and was about to get it finished.

Leaving young Timmy to play by himself, big Tim joined the grownups, getting himself comfortable in his chair nearby. For a moment he just sat watching his mother. Her yarn ball kept unrolling as she incorporated that yarn into her work. He asked her, "What'cha making now. Mother?"

She looked up, smiling at him, never missing a stitch, "Mittens for the kids. Winter'll be coming one of these days and we'll need to be ready."

Before sitting down, RoseMarie had picked up her knitting bag. Getting herself all arranged for the evening in her chair by Ethan, her agile fingers were making those knitting needles fairly dance. Using dark yarn that would hide some of the children's soil, knitting mittens was a pleasant task. As those needles clackity-clacked she was envisioning the fun and laughter of the children with the snowball throwing and the sledding. She could feel that happiness from her own childhood, and when memories of that excitement raced through her, her fingers went even a bit faster.

Listening to the others talk, she made the last tie-off of a finished mitten, then picking up the ball of yard, she said, "Timmy, Ruthie, come here to grandma for a minute. I want to measure you."

With the two youngsters standing at her knees, first with little Ruth, she held the yarn end to one wrist. Then she unwound yarn to take it across the back of the little shoulders and down to the other wrist. Cutting it off, she said, "My goodness, how you've grown. I'd better make this a lot longer; 'cause by the end of the summer you're going to be a big girl." A wide, happy grin spread across little Ruthie's face.

RoseMarie repeated this procedure on Timmy. Those lengths of yarn would be attached to each of a pair of mittens. When extended across the shoulders and left hanging out each coat sleeve, the mittens wouldn't get lost.

RoseMarie had several more pairs to make. With Mary Rose's two children along with these two, there would be need for extras, especially for the older ones.

By now, the logs had burned down to glowing embers and Martha had gotten the children settled in their beds in the loft. She was getting ready to call it a day herself.

Ethan said, "I'm not quite ready for bed yet. I think I'll just put on another log and sit here for awhile longer."

As he started to get up, Tim said, "Let me do it for you, Father." And he raked up the ashes around the embers and then carefully laid on a smaller log. It was warm enough outside that it was no longer necessary to keep a fire banked and burning through the night.

Finishing up, Tim and Martha said their "good nights." They went into their bedroom then, closing their door.

Intently watching this, Ethan remarked, "RoseMarie, it's a matter of fact, I can just see me. I am becoming my own father!"

Looking up at him, those needles never slowing, she said, "Well, Ethan, I believe that's the way it's supposed to be."

"But, my dear wife, not with us!" He seemed to say it more to himself than to RoseMarie. But also, he was studying about how to bring up what he'd been pondering about lately and he wasn't quite sure about just where to start. He was certain, however, that his plan was at the point of being ready for RoseMarie's opinion.

Looking at him, trying to read his face, she laid down her knitting, saying, "Ethan, you've seemed so quiet tonight like you're brooding about something. Is there anything wrong?"

"Well, you're right about the brooding but I didn't know it showed. No, nothing is wrong. But I've been thinking a lot lately. About us...about you and me." Ethan looked lovingly at RoseMarie. And then he was still for a moment.

Adjusting himself in his chair, sort of sadly he began, "You know things aren't the same without John. Of course, they're not the same for anyone after the war. I know we've all made the best of it and we've kept right on. And, of course, that's the way we should. Maybe it's been harder on us older ones. The kids all have their own busy lives. With their young families they've had to stay focused and keep busy." He paused.

He could see that he was making RoseMarie look saddened. John hadn't been gone quite a year yet and so many things like missing his place at the table caused gnawing pangs to flare up all too often.

But, now that he'd started with this Ethan wanted to keep on. Smiling ever so lovingly at her he began again. "Well, my precious girl, there's one thing that has not changed and that's my love for you! I can't begin to tell you how much you mean to me and how you've always made everything about my life so special."

And by that look on his face RoseMarie knew that he meant it. Throughout all their years together that same look had never failed in keeping her feeling as though she was very special!

He continued, "My dear Rosie, what would you think if I told you that through those busy war years and during these months since, I've been laying aside money...lots of money. I've used my share of the mill money to take care of our family needs but most of it I have stashed away in a safe place. Just letting it accumulate. That was easy to do because there hasn't been time for anything else but work anyway." He hesitated, watching for her reaction.

He could tell that she was interested, but she wasn't showing too much excitement about it. After all, each of them knew that family riches were not measured in money.

Ethan went on, "For the past few years now, I've been doing a lot of reading and doing a lot of listening to some of the people that have passed through our way. All the talk about the homesteading has really intrigued me, especially about over west in Illinois. In '62 the government made the Homestead Act into law. A man can choose a tract of land and get it registered as his own. The only requirement is that he must occupy it for a while."

"Ethan, what are you trying to tell me?"

"My dear, I'm telling you that I've been thinking about you and me going out to Illinois and homesteading a tract of land!"

His wife just stared at him. A startled expression had come over her face. It would be her turn now to think of why this was ridiculous, just like he'd had to do. Ethan had already been through all of that reasoning part himself.

With her just sitting quietly, trying to digest what he'd just proposed, Ethan went on, "Rosie, I've spent lots of time going over the 'cans and cannots' of this and my 'cans' have come out way ahead! I want you to think about it."

"Ethan, I don't need to think about it...we can't leave the kids!"

"But they don't need us. They're grown up into wonderful adults. They need to have their own space to raise their families."

"We could never leave John," she said sadly.

And Ethan said, "That's right, RoseMarie. We can't leave John. So, we'd take him with us...in spirit, that is. Always, John was so happy. He loved fun. He loved music. He never wanted to hurt anyone. Wherever he is now, he's still like that."

Ethan stretched his arm across to his wife patting her hand where it laid across the knitting in her lap. So very tenderly he said, "Rosie, you know that our John is not confined in that grave. When I think about our John, I like to imagine him as being close by. Sometimes I see him as a beautiful butterfly flitting so gracefully and quietly about, adding beauty and pleasure to every spot as he darts here and there." Squeezing her hand, he added, ever so lovingly, "They can always use another butterfly in Illinois, RoseMarie. So, you see, our John would be right there with us."

"Oh, Ethan, you're going to make me cry!" And RoseMarie squeezed his hand back.

"Honey, believe me, I've been doing a lot of pondering over this and I've sorted through all sides of it. There's no reason for us not to do it. We can afford it. If we get there and decide we don't like it, we can come back and go on with our life here. Tim and Martha can take care of this house. If we do like Illinois and decide we could make it there, then if any of the kids wanted to join us they'd be welcome. And with traveling being so much better and easier these days, if we wanted to, we could always come back here on visits."

With a hint of some of his old enthusiasm in his voice, he added, "Rosie, look at all the changes we've already been seeing. Well, there are changes yet to come that we can't even begin to imagine! Rosie, things are just going to get better and better."

Ethan's face was brightening up. He said, "You know, over the years when I would listen to my father and mother tell of their pilgrimage from Pennsylvania out here into this unknown country of Ohio, I always felt a little bit envious. And just look what bravery and their strong faith gained for them! And, whenever they do talk about it, I've always felt that I could detect some excitement about it that they still share."

RoseMarie just sat there for a moment. Quietly, then, she got up and walking to the sewing table nearby she laid her knitting work down. Coming back to her chair, she turned it a bit to better face Ethan. Then, sitting back down, she just looked at him, not saying a word. What a tremendous proposal he'd just laid in her lap.

Ethan reminded her of a little boy. There he sat, exuding an air of excitement, anxious, awaiting her approval. Just watching him she had to smile, shaking her head from side to side. My, oh my, how she loved him.

All those many years ago, when so eagerly she had promised to marry him, she had been certain right then that she was ready to leave the comfort of her parents' care to be with him for all of forever. All she would ever want was to be by his side. And, at that moment long ago back then, she had known for certain that she was ready to accept wherever that "forever" might turn out to be. She'd been so confident that he would provide for her.

Remembering now, deep down, she knew those feelings had only compounded with the passing of the years. Never ever had Ethan betrayed that confidence.

And with remembering that, a flash of that same old all-consuming love went washing through her and goose-bumpy shivers went up and down the skin of her arms. Ethan still did that to her. She felt her face getting warm. She knew she was blushing. She hoped Ethan wasn't seeing it.

But Ethan was seeing it! He saw that sudden mystical brightness that was reflecting from her face. With his eyes so closely watching her, trying to interpret her reaction, he saw that same rosy aura of glowing loveliness that always drew him to her. He had to push down the urge to jump up right then and take her in his arms. And he knew that later on, once they were in their own little curtained-off corner, side-by-side together in their bed, he was going to do just that.

RoseMarie was shaking her head, audibly making a little laughing sound. She was saying, "Ethan, Ethan, Ethan! What a treasure you are."

Then seriously she said, "You know, I've been feeling so sorry for you these last few months. You'd be here with us, but you'd be so quiet, not like your old self. You'd seem to be far away and lost in your own thoughts, and I believed it was because of your grieving for John. But Ethan, it's been about this, hasn't it?"

"Well, I do think about John a lot. I know we both do and we always will. But I've learned to make myself dwell on the happy times. You know whenever you were around that boy you could just feel your spirits lift. He made you feel sunshine even if it was on a dreary day," and the corners of Ethan's mouth were forming a little smile as he was remembering.

Pushing back a wisp of her hair, crossing her legs at the ankles and arranging the long skirt of her dress over them, she studied him for a moment. Then she said, "You have this all figured out don't you? You've already been making plans, haven't you? And if I'll just say 'Alright let's do it,' you're ready to go right now, aren't you?"

"Hey, that's three questions, Rosie!" But his whole face was smiling now. "Well, the three answers are 'Yes, I guess that's about right'."

Ethan was beaming. He hadn't really known just how RoseMarie would react to all this. After all, they had become quite solidly settled into this routine of their lives. He knew that he'd just given her a startling shaking up.

Being sensible as was his nature, he became serious. "My dear Rosie, I am 46 years old and you're right close behind me. Our kids sure don't need us to look after them any longer. But, also, I've been thinking about another thing." Here Ethan paused a moment as if arranging his thoughts.

He looked soberly at RoseMarie, then he went on, "That Bennett Mill is supporting each one of us Bennett families, and it's still doing a good job of it. But when I look at the forest I can see that it's taking a big toll on the trees to do it. There are a lot of us Bennetts, you know," and Ethan smiled with that.

Going on then he said, "When I first began to hear about this land in Illinois, I began to find out as much as I could about it. They say a good part of the state is flat land and it's easily tillable for growing good crops. They call it 'prairie land.' Just think, Rosie, since '62 the law says that a big-sized stake of that new land can be ours just for claiming it and then we'd have to occupy it for a length of time."

Then came that boyish enthusiasm again. He said, "I think it would be a fantastic adventure for you and me to just set out and do it."

"But, Ethan, it's a big country out there. How would you know where you wanted to go?"

"That's true," he said, "but I've been reading everything about it that I could get a hold of. I've talked to people about it and I've done a lot of thinking about it." Saying that, he rolled his eyes, shaking his head.

Then he said, "There's one place especially that I like the sound of. It's just a little way into Illinois over the state line of Indiana, and it's a place called Danville. They say it's grown into a pretty good-size town and it's the county seat with a courthouse. I heard that President Lincoln used to spend a lot of time there before he became president. That was back when he was still practicing law. He'd visit there with a Joseph Lamon and his family, and they'd invite him to stay at their home. They say that back in 1850 Mr. Lamon built one of the first houses in that town that was made with a framework of wood. I guess the president had a lot of friends there in that town." Ethan paused a moment, looking at RoseMarie. Then he said, "I think I'd like to look around that area first."

RoseMarie was listening, but also she was closely watching him. She did like the livened-up look about his face. She knew the war years had been heavy for him. Lovingly, she smiled at him. And she did know she could trust him.

She said, "Ethan, you have your mind all made up. You're really set on doing this, aren't you?"

With that he gave her a sheepish-looking grin, saying, "My dear Rosie, all I'm waiting for is to hear you say 'Let's do it,' and look as though you mean it."

"My goodness, Ethan, this is so frightening. Do you know just what all you're implying?"

"Yes, actually I do. But do you know what, Rosie? This is the '60s. Things aren't like they used to be. It's not like those olden times when my father and my mother packed up and left their home in Pennsylvania. They came here in a wagon and there were no marked trails for them to follow. But today we have roads. Or we can choose to make the trip by train and there'd be a dining car with food and there'd be a sleeping car with berths for sleeping. Or we can go by the waterways." He looked at RoseMarie. "Tell me truthfully now, don't you feel just a little bit of excitement about this?"

Ethan was all smiles again. "It would be just you and me, my little Rosie, just the two of us. And, we'd be as free as two birds! No chores to do. No kids to attend to. We'd be seeing country that up to now we've only heard of or read about. We'd be having the chance for experiencing probably the biggest adventure of our lifetime!"

His face had become so alive, emitting the zeal he was feeling. It was so great to finally be getting to share all this with RoseMarie. And he just had to make her share in his enthusiasm as well.

Ethan got up from his chair and went over to the fireplace. He picked up the poker then stirred the embers a bit. As he laid on a couple of the smaller pieces of wood, he said, "Rosie, I'm wide awake, how about you?"

"You know I am. I'll not sleep for a week! So, have you talked of this to your father?"

"Not yet. First, I had to be sure in my own mind that we could do it, and then I had to hear what you thought about it. You just don't know how I've wanted to talk with you about this, but as I said, I had to be sure myself first."

He paused a moment, then continued, "Now I will speak with my folks. But, Rosie, you know my father. He will never be against anything that's important to us."

"Yes, I know. Both Caleb and Minerva have always been wonderful to me." She was silent a moment, then she said, "Oh my, we would miss being with all the family. Ethan, we've never been out of the shadow of our place here!"

"I know. I've considered that. But as I said earlier, if we were to find a spot we like and we made a new home there, it's likely that there would be some visiting back and forth. Remember things are getting easier all the time. And as I also said, if you and I don't like anything we see in the new country, we can come right back here and go right on as before."

He paused a moment, then, enthusiasm brightening his face, he added, "But, Rosie, I believe we would be all the wiser and happier for having done the traveling! I remember when I was just a little boy, reading of places far away. I always wished that someday I could go and see some of those places for myself. And, now, with my best girl at my side, I want to do it!"

"And have you already decided just how we would go on this venture?" Admittedly, RoseMarie was beginning to get caught up in Ethan's contagion and she needed to know more about what he had in mind.

119

"Well, I'd like to try the river. Those big paddleboats have always looked mighty enticing! Whenever one goes by the mill they sound fun. If we're outside people always wave to us. We can hear music being played and sometimes there's singing. We'd have a bed and there's a dining room. All we'd need to take with us would be our clothes and our main necessities." Ethan was that little boy again, getting all excited as he talked.

"Rosie, I've done a lot of thinking about this. We could go down the Ohio, on down beyond Newburgh where John was during the war. And where Carrie was at the Academy. We'd get off the paddleboat at the dock where the Wabash River comes into the Ohio. There'd be some kind of boat there that we could get on to ride up north on that river to Vincennes, Indiana."

Ethan stopped, and then excitedly he added, "It would be just like Major Sprinkle did at the turn of the century when he started his town of Sprinklesburg. That was years ago before his town was renamed Newburgh. And that was back in those old days before traveling became easy like it is now."

Ethan loved finally getting to voice all this out loud. Finally getting to share these dreams and ideas with RoseMarie.

Going on, "Then, my dear, once we got to Vincennes we'd go to a hotel for awhile. They say it is a big city now. We'd look around. And I'd buy a horse and a buggy." His face spread in a wide grin as he excitedly shared these plans.

"Then, our trip really would get interesting!" Ethan continued. "Once we got there in Vincennes, we'd be just a hop from the Illinois state border. So then in our new buggy we'd drive a bit to the west. And we'd pick up the old trail that President Lincoln had walked along when he was young. Just think, driving our new buggy along that same trail where Abraham Lincoln walked to help drive livestock to the big market in Chicago!" It was as though Ethan couldn't imagine anything so fantastic ever happening to him.

Continuing, he said, "We'd take the trail north to where it goes through the Danville area. And that's where I think I'd like to look for some land that we'd like for homesteading!"

"Oh, Ethan, really do you think that we can do all this?" RoseMarie could not believe she was hearing all this!

"Yes, Rosie, we can. I've thought it all through. And I want us to do it. We've always worked long and hard. Now, this is the first time that we are free enough to gamble like this. But, it's a gamble that I think will have a good outcome. Anyway, we can afford to do it and we have the time to do it as well." Pausing a moment, he added, "Like I said, if it doesn't work out we can come right back here and go on as before!"

"My goodness, Ethan, you make it all sound so easy." Now, she too was smiling. Definitely, Ethan's enthusiasm was contagious. And she had the utmost confidence in his abilities.

"Ethan, I swear, you have me feeling like a schoolgirl!"

"And you look like a schoolgirl, Rosie, sitting there all excited. We need to do this. It'll do wonders for both of us." Ethan smiled lovingly at her.

Becoming more serious, then, she said, "Ooh, the hardest part will be telling our folks and the children." She hesitated, looking at Ethan. "No, the impossible thing will be trying to get to sleep tonight in order to have the strength to tell the family!"

"Well, my dear sweet Rosie, maybe I can help with that. Right now, I have another plan. Let's get to bed," and then, lowering his voice so that only she alone could hear, he said, "I have a little workout in mind that might just make you tired enough to put you to sleep."

"Ethan!" This time, definitely, RoseMarie knew that she was red with blushing!

THIRTEEN

From Wisps to Format – 1866

Ethan sort of chuckled as he poked around the pieces of the burning wood, gathering them into a closer pile. As he worked, he was being careful not to disturb the big granite coffee pot perched there on the flat top of one of the rocks arranged at the edge of the fire. Satisfied, he laid on a couple more pieces of wood, taking them from the stack of small logs piled nearby. The pile included some lengths of split wood as well.

Close by, too, stood the little iron tripod. Now, the lidded iron pot suspended on it by its wire bail was all washed up from the stew they'd finished off at suppertime. And the iron Dutch oven was setting nearby, out of the way, probably empty now of biscuits. RoseMarie had made them to go with the stew. Glancing at that little iron oven, Ethan was remembering how tasty those biscuits had been.

"You're laughing, Ethan," RoseMarie spoke up from her chair where she was sitting just back a bit, away from the heat. "Tell us what's funny. Our friend, Billy, and I want to laugh with you!"

"Oh, I was just thinking. You know, I've sure stirred up many a fire over the years, but I still can't believe the fact that I'm tending this one clear over here in the state of Illinois! And that we're actually sitting here on this 160 acres of our very own!" Ethan just shook his head, saying "I just can't believe how everything has fallen into place letting all of this happen." He sat back down in his chair, there beside his wife. Their new friend, Billy Mitchell, was sitting there too across the fire from them. A slight evening breeze was trailing off the bit of smoke as it rose from the flames and disappeared into the dusky night air.

Billy's big collie, Buddy, was lying close to his feet. All stretched out, lazily, the dog was feigning sleep.

Ethan was saying, "I know, so far these are just empty acres that we have here but I'm visualizing the time not too far ahead when all of this is going to be a busy, thriving place. Before too long we won't be roughing it like we are now. Billy and I are going to see about getting a barn built. When we get it finished, then our animals, as well as us, can be inside. Temporarily, we can all live inside the barn and be out of the open weather." Ethan paused, his countenance busy in deep thought.

He went on sharing his thoughts aloud, "I've already sketched out just how I want our set-up to look. It's going to take some time, I know. We can't get it all done at once. But my plan is to start off first with that barn. Right from the beginning, when I looked at the whole big picture, I could see that this area around where we've made this camp would be the choice spot for our house and yard and the barn lot. It's close to the marked-off roadway, with the barn lot being a good place to put the road gate and a driveway."

As Ethan talked he was noting his wife. He was gauging her reactions, hoping she would become as enthused as he was. He went on, then, voicing his plans. "Maybe you two haven't noticed but there's a little hill out there a ways and it'll be the ideal spot for that barn. By using the hill, we can build a barn that'll be on two levels. And we'll make the barn lot big enough for a nice cow barn, a place for a few pigs, and whatever else we may decide that we need."

He stopped there, picking up his coffee mug from where he'd set it on the ground. Taking a sip of coffee, he was quiet for a moment, watching the flames.

Going on then, "By building the barn into that little hillside, it'll be easy to make a lower area for horses. Then by using that natural hill as an incline ramp leading up to a wide doorway opening, we can have a main floor over the lower part."

Again he paused, thinking a bit. "I want it to be a big barn with a nice hay loft above that main floor. Then, with the way this side of that little hill lays, with a little digging, we can level off a big space. And it'll be perfect for attaching a big storage room for holding straw. That side of the barn can set right on the ground."

Like an after thought, he added, "By putting in some partitions on that main floor, we can have some temporary living quarters. We can make do living there while we're putting up the house."

Again he paused, looking at his wife. With the gathering darkness settling in around them on that late May evening, the gentle evening breeze was keeping the flames of the fire flickering and glowing.

Sitting there, her work of the day behind her, she looked so contented. With the golden hues of the flames softly reflecting off her face, just watching her, just like always, Ethan was falling in love with her all over again! He just breathed in that picture. Right then that man could have moved a mountain!

Watching this scene, even young Billy was responding in pleasant contentment. He wasn't used to nor did he understand that specialness that generates from amiable, loving family. He just felt good, sipping coffee and smiling, absorbing that hovering serenity. At that moment he too could have kept up his end of any mountain moving!

With love and tenderness showing on his face, Ethan said, "Rosie, the house I'm going to build for you will be a dream place. I want it to be the palace that a queen like you deserves."

"Oh, Ethan, for goodness sake, I'm certainly far from being a queen!" But just hearing him say it made her feel all-pretty. Then, "Well, forgetting that part, I do believe you. How you do amaze me."

Then she added, "Anyway, this is a fun experience. It's so different from any life we've known," and the smile on RoseMarie's face was verifying her words. "My, how our children would love this."

"I know, Rosie. You're missing them, aren't you?" Then, to their new friend he said, "Billy, I've got me one brave woman here. But I'll bet you've already noticed that."

"Yes sir, Ethan, that I have. Let me tell ya, I'm sure proud to git to be a part of this venture of yours. I believe it was my luckiest day ever when Buddy and I met you that day over there in Danville," and he reached down to stroke Buddy's head. "I was just driftin', ya know, wonderin' what I oughta do next. And you come along. And here I am!" Billy sort of shook his head, his hand still petting his dog.

Right now he too was feeling thankful in that maybe he also was getting to take on a different way of life. And with the future Ethan had laid out for him, it was a new life that was appearing more and more to be quite agreeable with him.

For a moment the three of them just sat there quietly watching the fire and sipping their coffee. Each was holding one of the ironstone mugs from the set that RoseMarie had chosen at the general store back in Danville.

True to Ethan's original plan he and RoseMarie had left the Wabash River at Vincennes, Indiana, staying a few days there at a hotel. First, Ethan had bought the buggy and then began looking over the horses. He had to find one that was already "broke" to being harnessed to a buggy as well as for riding. And then he had spotted that sleek sorrel one. Stroking her head, talking softly to her, Ethan could sense an immediate bonding between the two of them. The owner guaranteed her to be a gentle rider and he assured that she would do well standing between the shafts, hitched up for pulling the buggy. Ethan told RoseMarie that once they were settled, this was to be her own horse and buggy. That pretty horse had already been named "Fannie" and Rosie claimed that the name fit her very well.

Then, just as planned, they'd made their way over west a bit, crossing into Illinois. Finding the now well known Lincoln Trail, they took it on north to the town of Danville.

Just as Ethan had been told, Danville was the local governing seat of the county and it was just a few miles inland from the Indiana line. Also as Ethan was expecting, that Lincoln Trail went right along the town.

Once there, again they set up in a hotel. RoseMarie would be comfortable there resting and she could have a chance to look around.

Ethan, taking Fannie and the buggy, set out to look for his piece of land to homestead. He had picked up some necessary provisions, like a bedroll for sleeping at night along with some hay and oats for the horse. He had a coil of rope for tethering

Fannie and some items of food for himself. Also he'd made room for a wash pan and a piece of soap cut from the store's big homemade block. With a big box of household matches and Mother Nature's ready supply of wood for making fires, Ethan knew he would do just fine.

RoseMarie had spent her next days like a pampered lady. But in case that Ethan did find a suitable piece of land, she had noted a store that carried items she knew they would be needing for their period of primitive-style camping out.

Diligently, but excitedly, Ethan searched for his quest. Within a few days, he returned, ready to hunt up the Claims Office. He had discovered their perfect place.

It was an available one-quarter of a section of land, the allowable 160 acres. It was tillable and within 20 to 25 miles a bit north and west of Danville. There was even a small pond on it with clean, pure looking water. The entire section that included Ethan's acres was squared off and bounded along the one side by faintly marked wagon tracks cutting through the prairie grass.

It was an elated Ethan that had rejoined his wife! To RoseMarie he was a new, rejuvenated Ethan. And she was ready to be his full partner.

It was during the dickering while buying a necessary wagon and a team of horses that Ethan met Billy Mitchell. He was taken with the young man right from the very beginning. Billy reminded him of his own son, Tim. He looked to be a bit younger than Tim. And although he looked somewhat weather worn and rough, Billy came across as being honest and trustworthy. In their general conversation the boy had appeared to be level headed, even quite knowledgeable, and Ethan liked his gentleness with his dog.

Ethan had invited Billy to join them for supper in the hotel dining room. He wanted RoseMarie to meet him. He himself had begun to realize that he could use some good reliable help in getting squared around with this new project. And he wanted to get her opinion of Billy.

Happily, those two had hit it right off. Not only did Rosie like Billy, but she felt comfortable with him. And, to Billy, RoseMarie was like getting to have a mother. He couldn't remember ever having a mother of his own.

From that suppertime on, Billy became a part of them. Ethan took the young man under his wing, booking a room for him close to his own. He took Billy to a dry goods store, buying him some extra clothes. Although Billy was already accustomed to a primitive outdoor life, Ethan wanted him to have several changes of clean clothing for those next days. He had plans for Billy's taking a major part in the procedures that he was visualizing taking place.

Ethan's mind was busy with plans for the days ahead. That open-air style they were going to be living was going to be rugged. It was going to be void of their usual comforts and facilities. But Ethan couldn't see any other way.

RoseMarie liked to watch Billy eat. The boy had a healthy appetite. He drank his coffee black and he ate a lot of bread. He'd drink down about a third or so of the cup, then meticulously he would measure out just the right amount of sugar, stirring it into the cup. With each piece of bread, then, carefully he broke off the crust and he immersed that crust into his remaining coffee. By the end of each meal that cup would be filled with coffee-soaked bread crusts. Billy, then, with his spoon, would finish it off, ending with a look on his face of happy satiation.

Now, Billy, along with his own enjoying watching the fire, was also studying about Ethan. This man seemed to have some major work in mind. What he had laid out so far was not kid stuff. And yet, here they sat with no visible tools or means to work with. And Billy began to voice that out loud. "Ethan, tell me just how are we going to go about all this?"

Ethan chuckled. "Well, Billy, my boy, for some time now back home over there in Ohio, I have sat looking into evening fires, doing a lot of thinking. Watching a fire has always held a fascination for me. Watching those wisps of flame and those tendrils of smoke drawing toward the chimney of the fireplace, or around an outside fire like this, has always had an effect on me. It has had a way of making me dream of things. And the more I dreamed, the more and more those dreams looked to be attainable. Especially my dream of having a place like this one right here."

Ethan stopped to take a long drink of his coffee, then he continued, "The dreaming part was easy. But once I put this dream plan into words it became a different story. Now, I've got to put my words into action!"

Ethan looked at the two of them sitting there listening so intently. And for just a fleeting of an instant a sinking sensation washed through him. He felt like that kid again when he used to boast of something and then had to produce on it to save his reputation. Sometimes, all throughout life, he'd felt this was a character flaw. Like if ever he would just keep his mouth quiet, then if something became too difficult he wouldn't be committed to carrying it through.

Like now...take this project. It was so reachable in his dreams. But, once putting it aloud, he was really committed, big! Just at little fleeting times even he questioned just how he was ever going to get it all accomplished. Just how was it all going to turn out?

But, just like in those other times, that doubt never lasted for long. He took a few more sips of his coffee, watching that fire. And he became that positive Ethan again.

He did feel a bit sheepish, though. *"My God,"* he thought, *"I hope none of what I was just feeling was showing on my face!"* He sensed that he had just let down his defenses, exposing some of his real inner self. He realized that maybe he'd allowed these two to witness this weakness in him. He couldn't have that happening. They were looking to him for leadership. But he knew RoseMarie had faith in him. She had always trusted his judgment. Even the whole family, although shocked at first, had accepted this venture as a fact that was going to happen.

He breathed in a chest full of that pleasant evening, mixed now with the assurance that he would make this become the reality just as it was in those dreams. Having come this far with his plans, he was ready now to share his ideas for the next steps. He was the old Ethan again. He began to smile confidently.

Beginning, he said, "Billy, I mentioned to you about my family's lumber mill and the forest of trees. Well, when we get ready to build the house, I want to bring our own lumber from the mill. For the other buildings, we'll use lumber from local supplies. First, we'll have a well put down. Then, once the barn's finished, we'll put up the cow barn and a chicken house.

And we'll have to have a garden." Billy gave a little whistle. And he let out a "Whew!"

"Uh, huh," Ethan agreed, smiling at Billy. "I said my 'whew' at first, just like you. But, I've had plenty of time to work through all that."

Billy asked, "Just how long do we have to get all this done?"

"Well, I'll tell you. I've thought long and hard about all this," and saying that, Ethan got up, going over to the coffee pot setting there on the flat rock.

First, using a finger to test the handle, he took a piece of rag from his pocket. With one hand he held a portion of the rag around the hot handle and with the other hand he used the rest of the rag to support the lid.

In answer to his companions' nods he filled their empty cups, then his own, replacing the pot again on the rock. All the while he was quiet as if in deep thought.

Back in his chair again, glancing at Billy, "I realize that I was born into a nice heritage made possible by hard-working conservative parents. Without that I'd never have the chance even to consider any of this. Well, Rosie and I have done some hard work too, so now, financially there's no reason that this can't all happen."

Again he paused, then "The way I figure it, in the long run, this whole thing right up to the finish is going to cost just so much, no matter how I go about it. So that gives me two options. One is to drag it out, taking on one project at a time. Or I can hire enough capable men all at once, hiring small crews to work on each part of the overall plan at the same time.

That way we'll get it all finished at once." Again, he stopped to take a sip of coffee.

His next statement was, "Then, I want to head up our farm. This is farmland, you know!"

Again Billy whistled and again he said, "Whew!"

RoseMarie just drank from her cup of coffee.

After studying a moment, soberly Ethan looked at his wife. "Now, my dear Rosie, you've heard all of this. It's time to stop right here, right now. I want to listen to what you think about all this. And, Rosie, I mean what you REALLY think! You and I are in this together, you know. So now, before we go any further, it's time for you to make a choice. It's all up to you. Shall we get hammers and nails or should we just walk away from the whole idea?" He laughed, saying, "Well, no, we wouldn't walk. We'd hitch up Fannie to that buggy and we'd trot back home."

With that Ethan smiled warmly at his Rosie, waiting. He was sincere in wanting to hear her opinion.

Quietly, she drank some more. She, too, was studying that fire.

Then she looked at Ethan. Emotions were welling up within her. What an amazing man she had married! And in all those 29 years of their marriage, he'd kept their togetherness so alive. But this adventure with all the change it presented was pretty overwhelming. She was so proud of him. And she harbored no doubt but that he'd be able to carry it through. She wanted nothing else but to be right here at his side, helping him to see it all happen just as he was planning. And, waiting there, watching her, Ethan was seeing his answer lighting up her face!

She verified it out loud. "It's going to take a lot of hammers, Ethan. We might as well get a whole keg of nails, maybe two!"

Again, Billy just whistled!

By now the darkness of the night had closed in around the little group. But excitement was helping to fuel that fire. The flames were licking at the wood here and there; giving off a crackling sound and now and then a shooting spark or two would pop up into the air. The embers edging the ring were glowing, adding their effect to the scene.

Now and then from one or another of the trees a screech owl would make a comment. And a movement or a snort from one of the horses tethered nearby blended in with those noises of the night.

Ethan declared, "I swear, I never knew a man could feel so happy!" Then he looked across at Billy, saying, "And what about you young fella? Still want to be a part of this?"

"Oh, yes sir! I want to tell you, I've never met people like you two before. You couldn't drive me away!"

"Well, then it's settled. And we need to get started." Ethan was all business again. "Billy, the law states that we must occupy this land in order to keep the claim. Again, I've already been deciding on the best way to get all this going."

Soberly, he looked across at this young fellow that he was liking better with the passing of each day. "I'd like to make you a foreman and have you stay here alone for awhile, just camping out like we are now, watching over the place. How about it? Could you handle that?"

Billy straightened up, mulling that over for a moment. Ethan was laying trust in him, and he was ready to respond.

"Yes sir. You bet I can do that. You just lay out my orders and I'll see to them with all the best that's in me!"

"All right, foreman!" We'll start you tomorrow. Let's see now, I can get good men at a few cents a day plus their board. But I want my foreman to be an extra good man, so you'll get board, such as this is for now, and 60 cents a day. How does that sound, Billy?"

"I couldn't ask for anything better, Ethan. I'll make you that good man!" And he smiled agreeably. Then, grinning, he added, "And Buddy'll be cheap. All he'll want is board!"

The three of them laughed happily.

Ethan said, "Alright then, that's settled. As soon as we get all squared around here, Rosie and me'll pack up some of our clothes and you can take us in the wagon to Danville. Rosie can wait at the depot while we tend to loading some hay and some feed for the horses. And we'll need food supplies for you, along with whatever else you think you'll be needing."

Then Ethan turned to his wife. "Rosie, I'd like my father and mother to join us here. Father has put the work of the mill mostly in the hands of my brothers anyway and I believe it would do them good to have a change for a while. You know my father is one of the best when it comes to building and Billy and me'll be needing all the help we can get!" Ethan felt good, smiling, just thinking about his folks.

Then he continued, "We can take the train from Danville and go back home long enough to get my father and mother talked into the notion of coming back here with us. I just don't believe that'll be too hard to get done! And, we can see everybody again." Gosh, it felt so good, just saying these things out loud.

Then, "Billy, this should take us less than a month. That'll put us into June. When we get back to Danville, I'll buy another team and a flatbed rack wagon. We'll be needing it anyway. Then we can haul back the extra things, like bedrolls for the folks, some bigger cooking pots and stuff to cook in them. And, we'll have to have some more chairs." As an afterthought he said, "It might even be a good idea to tie a milk cow or two behind that rack wagon."

"Ethan, you sound so certain that Caleb and Minerva will be coming." RoseMarie smiled at him. Then wistfully she added, "That would be so nice for us as well as for them." Mentally picturing that, her spirit livened. She said, "Well, hey, this is beginning to look like we'll be having an exciting summer!"

Billy had been doing some thinking on his own. "Boss, it sounds like there's going to be some busy times just ahead. And I can see that means there'll be lots of evenings of sitting around fires like this. There'll be resting, talking and planning. Now, the way I see it, it would be a good idea to have lots of wood ready for those fires. So, that'll be one thing I can keep busy at while you're gone...cutting down a tree or two, sawing it up and splitting firewood. We're going to be needing a big stack, you know. And I've got my gun. Maybe I can bag a rabbit or a turkey to be simmering in that pot while I keep that axe swinging." Then he grinned at RoseMarie, saying, "I'm a pretty good cook. Living as I have, I've had some practice."

And she smiled back at him, in agreement. "I believe you, Billy. You don't look a bit underfed."

As the three prepared to turn in for the night, Billy said, "It's my turn to keep the fire going tonight," and as he was saying it, he was rolling a big log over, sticking one end of it into the flames. In that position it would burn more slowly, lasting longer.

While keeping the area lighted for comfort, night fires also helped in warding off any animal that might be lurking inquisitively. At times during the night, then, when Billy would awaken, he would keep pushing the log a little further into the flames.

At last Billy was in his bedroll just outside the edge of the ring of light. Ethan and his RoseMarie were in their bedrolls, side by side, over across the area and also just out of that ring of light.

They had all gotten quiet, all settled down for some needed rest. It was comforting knowing that collie dog would be serving as a watchful sentry.

But each of those three heads, as each settled there into its pillow, was anything but ready for quieting down. Each with the iters of its mind pumping with speculation, was concerned with its own involvement in those plans that had circulated around that evening fire. There just was no inducement toward sleepiness.

FOURTEEN

Full Steam Ahead

"Oh, look! Quick…out there…twin fawns with the mother deer!" Minerva called out loudly.

Looking out the train car window, the others smiled. They could see the doe grazing on the grassy flatland while her young offspring were playing around her, leaping and running.

"Aren't they pretty," she stated more to herself than a question. "No matter how often I see deer, I never fail to get excited."

"Morning time like this makes those young guys feel foxy after a good night's sleep. I agree with you, Mother, they are pretty and they are nice to watch," Ethan chimed in. "You know, I even feel kind of foxy myself after my good night's sleep. How about you, Father?"

"Yes sir, my boy, I do. And this plate of ham and eggs is gonna keep me that way. It's a fact, I'm gonna have to watch out or traveling like this is gonna spoil me. I swear I think I could soon get used to a life like this!" Caleb looked happy and contented. "I don't know what's ahead, but right now, I'm glad you talked your mother and me into this wild undertaking."

Quietly cutting off a bite of ham, raising the forkful toward his mouth, Caleb looked across at Ethan, studying him. With his fork momentarily suspended, soberly, slowly, he shook his head from side to side. Resting the bite of meat back on his plate, he picked up his napkin, wiping his mouth. Looking at his son, "My boy, can you even begin to guess how much I trust you?" Then he smiled, laying his hand over Minerva's, eating there beside him.

"That was one afternoon in my life that I'll not soon be forgetting. When you told me the real reason you and RoseMarie had made the trip back to Ohio. Mervie and me were so happy to see you. We thought you were homesick for the kids and us. But, no, that wasn't it at all. No...you asked if we would just pack up a few things and take off with you! Just like that. You put us back in Pennsylvania in 1808 when we'd done that very thing. Only this time we were a bit more settled." Giving his head another shake, Caleb smiled. He picked up his fork, this time putting the ham into his mouth and he began to chew the meat.

"Well, Father, all I can say is 'thank you'," and the expression on Ethan's face verified that sentiment.

The four of them were having breakfast, sitting at a table in the dining car. Even though they were a couple of cars back from the engine and coal car, they had to raise their voices a bit to be heard over the rumbling of the engine. The train wheels lumbering along the rails beneath them were confirming and adding their bit to the whole effect.

Caleb was right. Successfully, Ethan and RoseMarie were returning from their mission to the Bennett glen in Ohio. In just a couple more days they'd be joining Billy Mitchell on their newly homesteaded land near Danville. And these four were about to launch into a challenge unlike any they'd ever before confronted.

Just as Ethan had hoped for, even being pretty confident that it would happen, Caleb and Minerva had consented to join them, to help them in getting a homestead set up on that new land.

Going on with their eating, enjoying the well prepared breakfast, Ethan commented "Father, I know what you meant when you said you could become spoiled by this kind of living. RoseMarie and I like it too. Life in the old days was never like this, was it?" He grinned at Caleb. "Do you realize we're going to be pulling in to the station at Danville by suppertime? And we left the Cincinnati station only a few days ago."

"You'll like it in Danville, Minerva," RoseMarie was quick to say. "We'll go to the hotel for tonight and we can indulge in a nice bath. I'm looking forward to that. And, come to think of it, we'd better take a good bath because it will be our last one for goodness only knows how long. Ethan and I have become pretty well seasoned drifters out there on our new land, but handy accommodations are almost non-existent. And it's going to be like that way for a while."

It was Ethan's turn to bolster some assurance in his parents. "Mother and Father, we can hardly wait for you to see our place. You're going to love it. You'll see its possibilities. And you'll also see why I needed you two. We just can't stress enough how Rosie and I need you to be right there with us. With your support and your guidance we're going to be on top of the world!"

"Well, son, I'll tell you the truth on that. Your mother n' me must have talked most of the night when you and RoseMarie first arrived back there at the Ohio glen. When you laid all that outlandish plan in our laps." Caleb paused a moment, vividly remembering.

"Part of us was excited and ready to go. But the other part of us couldn't see how we could just up and tell the family we would be leaving them....that we didn't know when we'd be coming back."

"Yes, I know, Father. Rosie and I went through that same thing before we ever started with this. But now tell me...all this is exciting isn't it?"

"Let me answer that, Ethan," Minerva spoke up. "I swear this is making a new man out of your father. He's got a new spring in his step. I keep looking at him, watching to see if his gray hair is turning dark again."

"Well now, tell me, Mother, don't you recognize someone else that's doing some springing on her own?"

Minerva grinned at her son. "That's because I have to keep up with him!"

"Uh-huh," and Ethan reached across the table, patting his mother's hand. "You two will never know how indebted to you I feel. I can't tell you how much I'm looking forward to the months ahead. I know we'll all be working hard. But we're going to have a good time too. Our flat land doesn't look a bit like the forest glen in Ohio. We don't have the trees and we don't have the river. But we do have the peacefulness and the wide, open space that reaches across the land. Oh yes, we do have a pond which I hope to get stocked with some fish."

That brought a chuckle. And momentarily they each thought of the big blue Ohio water. It was a part of their life and had been for many years.

Caleb picked up the remaining biscuit half laying on the edge of his plate. Smiling, slathering butter over it, adding a spoonful of apple butter, aloud he asked his wife, "Mervie, does this jolt your mind a bit, having our own little room with berths to climb into for sleeping while we're traveling so effortlessly across the miles? All those years ago when we left Pennsylvania to head out into God knows what, we sure never dreamed that a day like this would come, did we?"

"I know, Caleb. I've been thinking that very same thing as we sit out there in the day car. Our children just don't know how good they have it, do they?"

Taking a swallow of coffee, a dreamy look about her countenance, she added, "It's so strange not to be working. I can't help feeling guilty in idling away the time like I'm doing. But I know that our Carrie is taking care of everything back home. I wonder if I can learn to allow people to wait on me... to sit here like this without having the urge to get up and wash these dishes." She sighed, shaking her graying head.

"I know, Mervie. I've been going through the same thing. But, like you, I know the boys are running that mill and taking care of things just the same as if I'd never left."

Ethan glanced at RoseMarie. She, too, was smiling. He finished cleaning off his plate. Picking up his coffee cup, sipping, he was quiet, doing some thinking.

Aloud he shared with them, "Well folks, like Rosie said, we'll get a good sleep tonight. In the morning you two ladies can do some store shopping and Father and I will buy that new team and rack wagon like I'd planned in the beginning."

Pausing to drink some more coffee, Ethan's mind was doing some mulling. Then, "It will take awhile to gather up all the gear that I know we'll be needing. We'll be living like gypsies for quite awhile, and we want to fair as well as is possible. We should be ready by tomorrow night so that we can start out bright and early the following morning. I'm getting anxious to get back out there and see how Billy and his dog, Buddy, are doing. He's supposed to have an enormous woodpile accumulated."

Chuckling, picturing Billy, he added, "So we'll be staying in the hotel a second night."

"Sounds like a plan to me, son. It'll be a change. Mervie and me'll be ready to revert back to those days of long ago when we first settled on our claim in that wild unknown! Think you're up to that, ol' girl?"

"Ask me again in about a month or so!" and she flashed Caleb an impish grin.

RoseMarie and Ethan exchanged happy smiles. They could see the pleasant acceptance of the older folks in their handling this change.

Suddenly Ethan's exuberance was charging the air around that dining car table. "I can't wait! Once that wagon is loaded and we're on our way out of town, in no time at all we'll find ourselves on that famous Lincoln Trail. We'll be on it for a few miles until we have to turn off on a little road to go a bit farther west."

At this point he hesitated a moment, then, "I guarantee you, once on that trail you're going to feel like you're a privileged person. Like you are traveling on hallowed ground. You may even feel some goose bumps just knowing you're actually being swathed in the greatness of President Lincoln. You'll sense it all around you! In the footprints you know are imbedded in that dust. I know I always do."

The little group was impressed. They were feeling a warmth….a specialness. Minerva spoke for all of them. "Son, already I can feel the privilege. What a wonderful summer we're going to have!"

And the waiter, coming along the aisle in his immaculate white starched coat, stopped to refill their coffee cups.

FIFTEEN

Wisps into Reality – 1869

Meticulously holding the rasp at just the right angle, Ethan drew down across the tooth of the saw. Another sweep and he moved to the next tooth. He was about half done with this side and then he would turn the saw over, ready to sharpen the opposite side of those teeth. This was a crosscut, two-man type saw with a handle on each end.

Ethan was using the stile as a workbench, sitting on one end of the wide saw blade, with his feet resting on the bottom stile step. With the weight of his thighs steadying the saw and with the teeth edge extending out from between his legs and over the edge of the stile, he had a clear access to each tooth.

He did have to watch that he didn't snag his Oshkosh overalls as he kept readjusting his position on the saw. Those teeth could make a hole in a hurry. And by the time the saw sharpening session was finished, his skin just back of a hole could show some painful evidence.

Keeping all the saws and axes sharpened was not a particularly fond chore of Ethan's, but it had to be done. Even summertime took its toll on the wood stack. There had to be fires for the cooking and the water heating.

Right now the family was enjoying a September lull. The summer crops and a good part of the garden had been harvested. The Mason jars were full. Jams and jellies were ready in their jars and glasses. There was a 5-gallon stone jar or two filled with sauerkraut from the cabbage patch.

It was all these accomplishments that had prompted Ethan's father and mother to announce it was time to return to their own home. That decision had been made a couple of weeks ago. Along with the folks' continuing to help with the autumn work, they began with their preparations for making their trip.

Ethan's mind was busy with all this as he maneuvered that file across the saw teeth. He knew the time had come for them to go home. But he was feeling a big void. That void began earlier that morning when Billy and Carrie drove the team out the gate with the old folks and their gear on the wagon. They were heading for the train station in Danville.

Three fruitful years of tremendous accomplishments had been made since that day the wagon had brought his folks in that gate. Yes, of course, it was time for them to go back home!

Ethan was appreciating this September lull. The corn crop was waiting for a frost so the shucking would be cleaner when the ears were jerked off the stalks. And that frost might not happen yet for a couple of weeks. Now was a good time for the men to build on that wood stack for the coming Illinois winter.

It was about time, too, for RoseMarie and Carrie to be making some hominy. There were several steps involved in that procedure. During intervals between their other tasks, the men would bring in a few bushels of the field corn. Once the grains of corn were shelled-off the cob, the women would immerse the grains in some in lye water. This would soften the hard outer skin in order that it could be removed. Then came lots of rinsings in clean cold water for removal of any trace of lye. Next came the cooking and canning.

Now and then Ethan's folks liked the exchange of hominy for potatoes to go with their breakfast eggs.

Ethan looked up to see RoseMarie approaching him. She was coming down the path from the side kitchen door, and she was carrying a half-gallon stone jug and a couple of glasses.

As she neared the stile, built there next to the little gate in the wire fence that separated the yard from the barn lot, she was saying, "I don't know about you, Ethan, but I'm ready to sit down for a while and have a nice cool drink of water."

Seeing her coming, Buddy had gotten up from his place in the shade near the stile, wagging his tail, showing his approval.

Anticipating the little respite, Ethan said, "Well, what a good idea!" all the while getting to his feet and moving the crosscut back a bit to the barn lot side of the stile. Then, he sat back down on the step.

Reaching the stile, RoseMarie set the glasses on the top, and then poured them full of the cold water. Picking up hers, she sat down on the end of the top step beside Ethan. Giving Buddy a pat on the head, the dog stretched a bit, and then laid back down on the shaded grass.

The two sat quietly for a moment, appreciating the cool drink. It was mid afternoon and although the sun was shining there was that crispness of fall time all about.

Ethan breathed in deeply of that air. Smiling, contentedly, he said, "Rosie, can't you just smell all of this?" and slowly he breathed-in again. "Ah, Rosie, I can't get enough of this. Here we are sitting in the midst of a wonderful dream come true!" He paused, just happily savoring the moment.

"I know. All this is hard to believe," RoseMarie agreed. "But it's so quiet. Caleb and Minerva have been gone only since this morning and already I'm missing them." She gave a little laugh, remembering, "Wasn't it amusing to watch them this morning, winding up their final preparation for leaving? You could just see that they wanted to get started on their trip back home to Ohio, yet they seemed reluctant to climb on that wagon to leave. Billy and Carrie could see it too. Ethan, your mother and father had become a part of this place. Their three years here were a long time. There's just no way that we can ever repay them."

"You're right about that, Rosie. I'm sure they do feel like they are a part of all this. But I'm also sure that Billy and Carrie got them to Danville and to the train all right. And it was time for them to see the rest of the family again. They're going to see a lot of changes in everything since they've been away."

Taking a swallow of water, musing a bit, his face brightened. "Do you know what I'll just bet, Rosie? I'll bet the family back there in Ohio will agree that Mother and Father have changed too, and all for the better. I think that having a key part in all this big project here has done wonders for the two of them. Don't you think they both looked peppier and spryer than when they came three years ago?"

RoseMarie smiled, picturing Minerva and Caleb. "I believe you're right about that, Ethan. Even though they worked hard, all this was a pleasant challenge. We always had a good time of it. There was always excitement and we were always seeing so much being accomplished."

Ethan took a few more swallows of water, and then he just shook his head, remembering. "Three crazy years! And during those years we've all been so busy with the actual work that all we could do was drop into our beds every night. Then we'd depend on the good Lord to make us rested and fit for the next day so we could do it all over again. But yes, you're right. We did have fun."

"Ethan, I'm so glad you tackled all of it at once, just the way you did. I'll agree it was sure hectic while so much was going on, but I believe that in the long run you handled it just right." RoseMarie hesitated, giving a little laugh. "For a minute, just picture how all that was! Goodness, but we lived in chaotic bedlam for a while there, didn't we?"

Taking a sip from her cool glass, she went on, "You had a crew for each part of that huge overall plan. So, with you and Caleb overseeing the whole thing, Billy and one group were putting up the barn, then the cow barn, then the smaller buildings. Caleb was concentrating on the big project of the house with the crew you hired for that. Then there were the men putting in all of the fencing. And all the while you were getting all the trees ordered and hauled in, with the men getting them in place. And you kept bringing in animals as the buildings for them were ready. How in the world did we last through all that?"

Ethan chimed in, "Well, my mind was always picturing how it was going to be when it was all finished. I guess everybody else thought I was crazy. Like that mile of our road out there...I could see its being so beautiful with those long-life maple trees lining both sides of it. Not only beautiful, but so shady. And I knew we'd be wanting and needing lots of fruits for eating, so I wanted the orchard started as quickly as I could. At the same time, I knew we had to get fields ready for crops so we could start getting in some income."

He thought a moment then said, "You know, Rosie, I sure was tossing out money there for a while just as if it would last forever!" But then he added, "Of course, I had already foreseen that in my big overall dream. I knew how all that would be and I was prepared for it."

"I know, Ethan. I never was worried for a moment! But what an experience we had. When night came, everybody was so tired. But, you know, through out all of it, they always seemed to be excited." Then she had to laugh, saying, "All those bed rolls! The hired men were around their own campfire. And the rest of us around ours."

She paused and then added, "I'm surprised we aren't still hearing the echo of all those hammers and sledges bouncing about!" RoseMarie took a couple more swallows of her water, smiling and remembering. "And, of course, there was Minerva and me along with Carrie, off and on at the times when she'd be here with us." Again, she paused a moment, "You know, at first, I thought that girl was excited about this place, the way she kept making those train trips back and forth from Ohio. I thought she wanted to be here and be a part of it. But I soon figured out that it was Billy that was causing all her excitement." Just talking about that made RoseMarie's face take on a happy look.

Then she continued with her description of that busy time. "We women would no more than get cleaned up after one meal when it was time to have another one ready! Bless little Carrie. When she was here she was so full of energy. She was such a big help. Let me tell you, it was nice to get moved into the main floor of that barn before that first winter." Again she paused, taking another drink.

"So you see, Ethan, that beginning plan of yours was quite ingenious. You had taken time in the beginning to get that all laid out in your mind and, voila, look what happened! This fantastic place got all finished!"

RoseMarie glanced around, taking in that whole picture. There was the yard in front of her with all the paths through the green grass and the beautiful gray with white trim clapboard house. A swing of her head to the left showed the maple trees lining the roadway with the farm gate closing off the worn dirt driveway coming up that end of the barn lot. Peripherally, then, to her right was a glimpse of the garden and the poultry set-ups.

"Yes, my wonderful husband. It all got finished. The buildings are up. All the trees are set out and growing so healthily. The buildings have livestock. The fences are run, marking off the yard and barn lot, the pasture, the orchard, the garden, and the fields for the corn and the grain.

RoseMarie stopped. She exclaimed, "Whew-ee, Ethan! You're right. We are sitting here in the midst of a dream come true!" She took in a deep breath. "It's fantastic the way everything is producing. When you look at this place you'd think all this has been here for years!"

Now it was Ethan's turn, "Yes, look at us now! Remember that neighbor who stopped off the other day as he was riding by? He told me everybody around this area is calling this 'the show place of the country'!"

Taking another drink of water, Ethan looked pleased about that. Then he said, "Rosie, we are living here like a king and a queen! At last, my dear, and I know you agree, you do have your palace," and as he said it, his free hand made a sweeping gesture toward that huge three-story home setting there in the middle of that big yard.

He squeezed her hand, lying there on her lap near him. "Rosie, just take a big whiff of this special farm air. We are farmers now, you know!"

RoseMarie turned a bit to better look at him. Her own face was showing love and contentment as she humored him by doing as he suggested.

As her chest expanded in a slowly drawn deep breath, Ethan asked, "Can you smell it...the good clean fall air, all blended in with the fruitiness of the orchard along with all the other good farm odors?"

It was true. The big orchard, all neatly laid out in rows, was growing on the opposite side of the house. And the fruit trees, even though still young, were this year producing a fairly nice crop. Now they were emitting into that air a definite proof of their presence, both through the ripening ones yet hanging for picking, but especially through the dropped, mushy ones laying on the ground under the trees.

The barns, both the one for the cows as well as the main barn for the horses, were giving off their particular odors, even though the animal quarters were being kept cleaned out by the hands. Also the hay in the loft and the straw in its barn were doing their part in counter balancing.

Then there were the pigs, the chickens, the ducks, and the little flock of turkeys. And just at that very moment, behind them on the barn lot side, there was a raucous uproar from a gaggle of geese waddling by. Those geese were registering a complaint about the stile's being closed off to them. Normally they would be hopping over it and into the yard where the grass was green and tender.

Geese and ducks were quite irksome with their dirty droppings, but when any one of them was all roasted, browned and savory- looking on a serving platter, all that was forgiven.

In the background, coming from the garden area, they could hear the muffled voices interjected now and then with bits of laughter from the two remaining hired hands, Alvie and Pete. Those two were busy at digging and cleaning off the potato crop, getting it ready for storing for the winter months ahead.

Otherwise, to Ethan and RoseMarie, the afternoon seemed unusually quiet. RoseMarie put her thoughts about this out loud, saying, "Ethan, do you know this is about the first time in the past three years that there hasn't been busy doings going on here?"

She paused, taking another swallow of water. "And do you know, for a while at least, it's going to be very different around this place. I'm going to miss having your folks being with us. I suppose by now they're well on their way back home to their Bennett glen.

"I can picture them right now, all relaxed, sitting there in their seats on the train, taking in the scenery. But I'll bet they're also thinking about home ahead of them. They never said as much but I'll bet they've really been missing all their family back there."

Thoughtfully then, "You do know, Ethan, really, there's just no way that we ever can repay them for their help in all of this. We are truly indebted to them," and she said this with genuine feeling.

"I know," Ethan agreed, "But they'd hardly been off their place in all those years from the time they settled there. I'm sure all this has done them a world of good. I always tried to shield Father from any heavy work, always telling him to just supervise and let the men do the labor. You know, Rosie, my folks are getting to be pretty old!" He paused a moment, as if that was difficult to believe.

Then, musing in reflection, he said, "Even though we were almost overwhelmed with all the aspects of the work, we have had a wonderful time, haven't we? Everybody always seemed eager to pitch in and do a good job. And as the whole place here began to take on a look of becoming an actual farmstead, everybody seemed to feel the excitement. I swear they worked all the harder!" Ethan was showing some of that same excitement in his voice.

"But you're right, Rosie, I don't think we could have done it without my father and mother. When we left here that first time on that train trip to Ohio, I had felt they might come for a while. But, just think, they've stayed here with us for over three years! I'll tell you, it was satisfying to have my father take over the supervising of all the building. He does excel at that. And Mother with all those extra men to feed! What meals the two of you turned out. She was a God-send wasn't she, Rosie?"

"Well, I couldn't have managed without her, Ethan. She never got upset. Like you said, though, I tried to do as much of the running and lifting that I could. But Minerva was always right there wanting to do her part."

Smiling then, remembering those confusing first days, having to make do under such limited conditions, she said,

"Well, your mother always knew just how to make a tempting pot full and those men all loved her."

"Well now, my dear Rosie, don't slight yourself in this credit department. You're a wonderful cook as well. I'll never forget you and Mother when all we had was out there in the open, living outside as we were. You two just contrived and managed, taking care of all us men. My God, at the biscuits you two kept turning out!"

"Oh yes, the biscuits!" RoseMarie shook her head just thinking about it. "They were pretty good weren't they? Once in a while some would be a little heavy but the men said those stayed with them longer! Anyway, it was surprising how those iron Dutch ovens baked so well. With the hot coals laying on the lids and just enough embers underneath the pots, those biscuits browned, top and bottom."

"You and Mother always both acted as though you were having a lark." Ethan remarked relishing those memories.

He went on, "I'll never forget when the barn was finished and we got all set up in there, one would have thought you two had discovered the pot of gold at the foot of the rainbow!" Ethan laughed.

"Well, it was nice to get moved inside out of the weather, Ethan. I remember those rainy times were very hard to deal with. But, while we're remembering, let's not forget our Billy Mitchell. That boy! Who would ever have guessed, on top of everything else, that he would marry our daughter and become our son-in-law!"

As Ethan did so often, he just shook his head from side to side. Then with sincerity in his voice, "Rosie, do you know, truly we have been blessed. Billy and our Carrie were made for each other. And now, here they are, married, living in with us and now they're going to give us a grandchild."

Again, he squeezed RoseMarie's hand. Then he added, "You do know they both love this place as much as we do."

"I know they do, Ethan. And I agree with you. We've been very, very blessed." She was still for a moment, thinking, remembering. Then she said, "When our little Carrie, that happy wonderful teacher, first announced that she and Billy were going to get married, I had a lot of mixed thoughts about it. I knew how she loved Ohio and I knew how she dearly loved her teaching work. But then, I began to remember about just what all takes place when a person falls in love," and, in that tender moment it was her turn to do some hand squeezing. And a knowing smile passed between them.

"Well, Rosie, in the very beginning of all this, during that very first fall time, when our Tim and Carrie both said they'd help, I was surprised. But truthfully, I was pretty happy about that. Getting all that lumber from the mill that I wanted to use for the house, and then getting it tied and secured on those river floats. And then helping me raft them down the Ohio to Cave-in-Rock down there in southern Illinois. I tell you Rosie all that was really quite an undertaking."

He paused a moment, smiling. "Then when Billy and the men had come down there in the wagons to meet us for the long haul on the trail back up here, I kept noticing the looks that were passing between Carrie and Billy, meeting there like they did for the first time."

Again he paused. "You know Rosie, I noticed another thing at that point back there at Cave-in-Rock. I believe that Tim was wishing that he could come on up here with us. But he knew he was committed with the other men that I'd hired to help him in getting the rafts back to Ohio. I was so fortunate in getting to make the deal where Tim could reload with goods back at that next port and get all of it back to Cincinnati. That helped a lot in covering my cost for that whole trip."

Here again Ethan stopped a moment. Then he added, "You know it won't surprise me a bit if someday Tim and Martha won't pack up their kids and manage to come over here for a visit with us." RoseMarie could detect a hint of longing in the voice that spoke those last words. It was a special moment there on that stile with all that reminiscing, all that remembering. And those feelings were accented by the pleasantness of that fall air with its gentle breeze.

All of a sudden RoseMarie straightened up, remarking, "Well Ethan, we're acting like supper and the chores will take care of themselves! Carrie and Billy are going to be pulling in any time now. And then we'll be stopping again to hear all about their trip to Danville and if the folks got all settled good for their long train ride. One thing, though, our supper table is going to seem empty with only the four of us now, along with only the two hired hands."

As she got to her feet, she was picking up the water glasses and the jug. Then, from habit, always thinking ahead to the next meal she said, "As for supper, I've got pie made but I've got to kill and dress a couple of chickens. Then there are the chickens to feed and the eggs to gather. And all the supplies the kids'll be bringing in will have to be put away."

Ethan agreed, then in a tone filled with tenderness he said, "Rosie, it's nice to have Carrie to help isn't it?"

"Oh, you bet. And I just can't wait to have our wonderful new house filled with baby sounds!" and her countenance showed it, beaming as she was in that anticipation.

Suddenly Ethan was remarking, "Well, speaking of sounds, do you hear a wagon coming?" And he turned to look down toward to road. Buddy was already down there by the gate, eagerly waiting. Being so used to Buddy, Ethan hadn't paid too much attention when the dog had jumped to his feet, scurrying up the steps and over the stile into the barn lot.

Ethan began gathering up the saw and the other gear. As RoseMarie had said, the evening chores were about to begin. Like the milking and attending to the animals. And the newly dug potatoes must be gotten in or the night would be filled with Buddy's barking as he policed the raccoons and rodents who would be trying to have a feast on them. Then there were the cobs to be gotten in for fire starting, the wood and the water tanks to be checked and filled.

Ethan always loved the evenings. There was so much peacefulness, such satisfaction, seeing to the safety and the comfort of the animals, all part of winding down the day. It gave him such a good feeling knowing his little kingdom was in order and running smoothly.

The team, on reaching that familiar country corner, had turned themselves onto that quarter mile stretch of maple tree-lined road. Although the trees were still young they were already tall enough to begin shading the heat from that western afternoon sun. And those horses, as well as Billy and Carrie, could feel the relief and began to pick up in energy.

Coming to the gate, again the horses knew to turn in, stopping. Handing the reins to Carrie, Billy alighted from the wagon, unlatching and swinging open the big farm gate. With a mere ripple of the reins in her hands, signaling, the horses pulled the wagon through. Then with Billy closing the gate behind them and he and Buddy walking alongside, Carrie drove on up the barn lot driveway.

Passing by the stile with an exchange of greetings with her parents, she drove on a ways, stopping at another wide gate in that same fence line.

Billy unlatched and swung open this gate. Carrie drove the team on through and followed along the well-worn wagon tracks that made a roadway running parallel to that northern yard fence line. This fence separated the poultry pens and the garden area from the yard.

There was an open place in the fence allowing Carrie to drive into the main yard and along close to the side of the house taking her to the back veranda area. There she called "Whoa" to the horses.

By that time Billy, Ethan and RoseMarie were there also and the unloading of the supplies for the house began. Billy and Ethan handled the heavy cloth-covered sacks while the women carried in the smaller bags like the several 5-pound bags of salt.

Billy carried in a 50-pound cloth bag of sugar setting it down on the floor near the sugar bin. That bin was one of several all built into the lower part of the wooden cabinet wall line-up. And midway of that wall Ethan had placed a door leading into a shelf-lined pantry. On the kitchen side of the door with the built-in bins along the lower part, glass-doored cabinets made up the wall above them.

Like Billy, Ethan set a 50- pound cloth bag of flour on the floor by the flour bin. Then some extra bags of each were carried into the pantry.

Later when the chores were finished and supper over, one of the women would have unraveled the seam thread along the tops of those two heavy bags leaning against those bins. They were ready, then, for the men to dump those contents into their bins. Again, later, one of the women would unravel the side seam and along the bottom of each bag, taking them outside then to shake thoroughly. The opened flat squares of cloth were then ready for washing. And with usage and several washings the lettering of the product brand name would have faded out. Or, for attaining softer whiter cloths quickly, a soaking in some mild lye water would bring that about.

Each cloth square was always put to good use, often for a dishtowel. Now, with Carrie's baby coming into the household, a special horde of these squares of cloth was slowly building. They were the perfect answer to the need for a supply of diapers.

Too the cloths were used in other ways, like in the making of cottage cheese.

That cheese procedure was pretty much an on-going routine. It just fit in with the normal day's chores. Quite often a big pan of milk would be left setting for a time on the very back, barely warm, part of the cook stove. This kept the milk at a slightly warm temperature and it would slowly separate into curds and whey. It was ready then to be dumped onto one of those squares of cloth spread across a big granite dishpan placed in the kitchen sink. The cloth ends would then be gathered up, tied tightly for squeezing, then hung up to allow dripping over the big pan. With the whey all dripped and squeezed out, the pan was emptied into the slop bucket setting on the floor near the sink area. And the curds were ready to be put through several clean water washings. With a little salt and some cream added, a supply of tasty cottage cheese was ready for the family's good eating.

With milk so plentiful and when the cottage cheese supply was ample, the poultry loved getting this healthful treat. They would peck at the curds and drink of the whey. The hogs liked the combinations also. When the slop bucket of it was dumped into their feeding trough, that trough got licked up clean as a whistle!

Now, setting the huge bag of rice he was carrying on a lower shelf of the pantry, Ethan smiled assuredly. He gave the bag a little pat, thinking, *there now, with the other bag out there by the bin in the kitchen we should have rice enough to do us 'til the early spring trip into town.*

Stepping out into the kitchen then and rounding the corner into the ell, he stopped by the sink. Picking up the tin cup, he pumped it full of water. As the cool well water refreshed him, he paused there leaning against the sink. And just as happened so often with him during quiet intervals like this, he began taking stock of his surroundings.

Surveying that length of distance from that wagon outside, across the big veranda, then coming through the outside back door and into the little foyer, on through the second door and into this ell, then on around to that ample pantry, the very spaciousness was awesome.

At once Ethan was filled with a sincere humbleness sensing how very blessed he was. He was very mindful of the fact that his and RoseMarie's little home back in the Bennett glen in Ohio wouldn't lack a whole lot of fitting into just this one big kitchen alone. And to think he and Rosie had raised a family back there in that little log house. Not only had they grown a family in it, but they'd always felt so fortunate that they'd enjoyed improvements not yet known when his folks had put up their own house a generation earlier.

The floor of that house of his folks was the original dirt that the house was built on. Way back then in 1808 a dirt floor was the commonly known practical method. But now, talk about improvements! Just look at this house! It was unbelievable!

This very sink he was leaning on was a good example. This kitchen sink setting here in the corner near the back door was a source of great pride. Swallowing the cool water, he was thinking of what a good job his father had done in building it.

Once Caleb had listened to Ethan's plan for it, Caleb himself had gotten enthused about the idea and he had taken over. But, he and his father both had needed to supervise that crew of men so closely. After all, those men, being common, had known only that water was gotten into a house by carrying it in a bucketful at a time. And the only way the wastewater got out was by carrying it out in a slop bucket. Or taking a pan of it to the back door and tossing it out across the grass!

It had been so amusing at times, noting those men's doubts about whether Caleb and Ethan had good sense!

First Caleb had the men build the wooden base cabinet, extending that base lengthwise to accommodate space for setting the hand-operated pitcher pump. An 8-inch deep, rectangular, open wooden box-like structure was built on the top of that base, leaving the one end of the base free for the pump. And about mid-center of the bottom of the box was the round drain hole to accommodate a 2-inch lead drainpipe.

The men had dug a long ditch beginning a few feet away outside the back doorway and ending several hundred yards away out in the orchard area. Then they'd lain 6-inch in diameter clay field tiles end-to-end along the ditch bottom to make a drainage system that would carry the wastewater under the ground. And the sink drainpipe ran down into this system. With the men placing some rocks in the ditch at the end of the tile, from there, the wastewater would become underground seepage. Ethan's men had put in this tile ditch covering it over with earth before any of the house went up.

Caleb had lined that wooden sink box with a thin, tin-like metal sheeting, amply over-lapping the seams, and he had ended up with this fantastic leak-proof sink. In all, it was about 40 inches long, 24 inches wide and 8 inches deep. It would accommodate a good-sized dishpan.

Next, the little hand-operated pitcher pump was set in its place there at the top level of the right hand end of the sink. The water pipe lead-in to the pump came up from under the floor, where it went through the brick-lined wall of a big underground freshwater vat.

Again, before the house was ever started, the men had dug out the pit and built this brick-lined vat, as well as laying the pipe underground that led to the new deep well out in the barn lot.

The house plan, then, included a nice-sized room with its flooring built over this vat. And that floor plan called for a 3-foot by 3-foot trap door to allow for maintenance service.

This room, adjoining the kitchen as it did, was designed as maids' quarters with a closet space. Its window looked out to the east, with a view of the little smokehouse that was built for curing meats. Also, the cob house, the garden and the poultry houses were out there in that same lineup.

Although Ethan and RoseMarie didn't yet have need for a maid, especially now with Carrie's living there with them, he'd thought ahead to the days when they got older.

Along with that vat for the clean well water, Ethan had a second vat built just outside at the back of the house, also brick-lined and underground. This vat lay under the floor of the foot wide boards of the veranda built out there at ground level, covering the back door area. This second vat was for storing rainwater with a pipe connecting from the eave downspout. Ethan's knowledgeable "well man" installed the hand-operated pump for that vat as well. The handmade soap made better suds for washing the clothes when the women used the rainwater from that vat. The soft rainwater was used too for bathing and hair washing.

Also while all this drainage system was being laid out, before any of the house structure was begun, Ethan had incorporated into the system two more drainage pipes. One of these came up to just a bit above ground level at a certain marked spot at the opposite house corner from the maids' quarters. Later when the actual building began, a small room was put here and a longer, higher rectangular wooden box was built. This box was placed right over that drainage pipe. Caleb had finished this box in the same fashion as he had the kitchen sink. And this box became a bathtub!

Now, by carrying hot water from the kitchen stove reservoir, cooling it just right with a bucket of cold water, a person could have a real bath. Such privacy was a luxury! Or, even when a quick bath would do, with using a small pan of water, a wash cloth and a piece of soap, even this was such an improvement over the old curtained-off place behind the heating stove.

Then, to fill that space in between the maids' quarters and the bathroom, Ethan's dream palace was sporting a "cooling room." This little room was unfailing in the responses it was causing.

From women seeing it, it drew "oohs and aahs," and Ethan could sense a degree of envy.

From the men he'd seen looks of amazement. Often he'd heard things like "Man, you are some kind of crazy!"

But RoseMarie was the one who mattered. And she loved it.

In the very beginning, when Ethan was looking for land to homestead, he had seen that natural pond with its clear water. No doubt it was fed from an artesian spring as was prevalent in that area. On seeing it Ethan's mind had begun to do some flip-flops. He'd begun to nurture a preposterous brainstorm concept.

Knowing of that area's winter zero temperatures, Ethan could envision that pond all frozen over with thick, hard ice. And he began visualizing how he could build a room to harness that cold for the summer's food cooling. He was confident that his concept was simple and workable.

He had the walls of that room built with a 6-inch space between solid sheeting of abutted foot wide boards. Then he'd had that space filled with sawdust. The walk-in door into the room was built in the same way but finished on the kitchen side as any regular door. A specially designed divider was put in at the ceiling level with the room space above extending up into the attic area.

This divider was built using thick lumber and well supported to handle the weight of the stored blocks of ice that would be filling that upper space. The upper side of the divider, which would be in contact with the moisture, was covered over with the same tin-like metal sheeting as the kitchen sink. And the divider was built slanting a bit to one corner where, again, the drainpipe led down to that underground drainage system… Ethan's third drainage pipe!

Ethan could envision that top storage space holding many big blocks of ice. The ice would have to be packed in very carefully and very tightly.

The room side of that ceiling divider was finished in the same way as the other walls. And the room itself was lined with some foot-wide board shelves for setting foods.

Once the house was finished, Ethan was looking forward to the freezing weather when he could test this icebox room. It had been so hard to wait for the ice to freeze thickly enough so he and the men could cut big blocks of it. Using the same method of 6-inch sawdust insulation, he'd had a trap door built up high in the side of the house. This gave access to that storage space. And with that area above the ceiling stacked with blocks of that hard ice, what a cool room RoseMarie had!

Late in the winter season with the ice covering the pond still good, he and the men restocked the blocks. With all that sawdust insulation, the coolness lasted 'way into the last of summer.

Truthfully he'd been anxious to see if this was going to be as successful in reality as it had become in his dream! Of course, with his rampant optimism, any lingering doubts were always short lived. His dreams were then free to keep right on soaring!

"I had to stop for a drink, Billy," Ethan explained to his son-in-law who was coming through the screened back door. Billy was balancing a gallon stone jug tagged "vinegar" along with a big bag of brown sugar plus a couple of smaller sacks.

"Water sounds good, Ethan. Three more jugs of vinegar out there and we'll be unloaded," Billy said. The jugs were some of their own which the kids had taken to town with them for refilling from the store's huge vinegar barrel. Billy added, "I'll have a drink too. Then I'll get the team taken care of and it'll be time to start the milking."

He grinned then, saying, "You know, along with that water, I'm going to get into the cookie jar. I've been thinking about those cookies and I believe a couple of them are just what I need to get me through the chores!"

"Our girls do turn out some pretty good ones, don't they? Maybe I'd better have a couple myself," and Ethan grinned at Billy. "But I'll go fetch those three jugs first," he said, already starting for the back door as he talked.

SIXTEEN

Ethan's Whispering Pines - 1869

"Mm-m, does it ever smell good in here," Ethan was saying as he walked in, going over to set down a bushel basket of red corncobs in back of the kitchen range. "I could smell it all the way from the cob house."

RoseMarie and Carrie were busy setting the last of the filled serving dishes on the big table centered there in the midst of the main part of the kitchen room. Both women smiled at him.

Carrie said, "Get washed up, Papa. Everything is hot and yummy."

She was leaning over that same beloved little worktable with its white porcelain rollers that Ethan had built when she'd been that little girl back in Ohio. Taking the last dish from off the top of it, she added, "Mom's done a good job on this platter of fried chicken. It and the hot gravy are probably what you're smelling."

And RoseMarie asked, "Are the others about done with the chores?"

"They're on their way in," Ethan answered, already at the sink, setting the wash pan under the pump and pumping water into it. Picking up the piece of soap he lathered his hands, washing them good and clean. Rinsing them off, he re-lathered them and began washing his face. Cupping his hands to hold water, he gave his face a rinsing, then stepped to the roller towel that hung from the wall at the end of the sink. Taking hold of both sides of the continuous toweling, he rolled it down a bit to expose some clean space. Pulling it to him, he dried his face and then his hands. Taking time to check himself in the little mirror above the towel rack, he turned to walk to his place at the table.

Reaching the table area he said, "Gee, Rosie, you're right about what you said earlier this afternoon. With only six places set here now this sure doesn't look like a table of ours!"

With the leaves still in place, extending the table to seat twelve or fourteen, it did look empty and different. But nothing was empty-looking about the quantity of food setting on it. This table was ready for some hungry men.

Besides the platter of chicken and the big dish of gravy to go over the mashed potatoes, there was the dish of home-canned green beans with pieces of bacon for flavoring, all steamy hot. Another dish was steaming with stewed apple quarters all syrupy and cinnamony, then the sliced fresh garden tomatoes and the bowl of sliced cucumbers and sweet onions swimming in vinegar.

And a hungry man could get his fill from just the usual things that always set in the middle of the table. Along with the filled cream and sugar bowls, the spoon holder, the vinegar cruet and salt and pepper were several opened jars. In them were pickled beets, bread and butter pickles, spiced apples, applesauce, jams and jellies, and apple butter. And there was churned butter to go on that plate of home baked bread. Also, of course, there was pie for topping off the meal.

All the work, beside the chores, gave those men ravenous appetites. Even the women, getting to sit, relaxed, their heavy workload temporarily behind them, were ready themselves for the partaking of some good victuals.

Footsteps on the back veranda announced the others. Each of those three was carrying a load of kitchen firewood. The two hired men, Alvie and Pete, placed their wood down, then went to the sink to get washed up.

Billy, laying down his wood, strode over to the table, letting out a cry of delight, "Mom, you made vinegar pie!"

"Well Billy, I knew after your long hard day that you'd be ready for a piece of your favorite pie." RoseMarie smiled fondly at him. "Anyway, that's about the easiest and quickest kind to make. Just boil up some water, sugar, a little vinegar, and thicken it. Add a taste of butter and sprinkle in some nutmeg and you've got pie!"

"I don't think I'll ever get filled up on pie, especially a vinegar one," Billy stated.

"And Carrie and I hope you don't," RoseMarie answered him. "Fill a man with a piece or two of pie and you've got a happy man. In fact, somehow pie has a way of making a whole room happy. Isn't that right, Carrie?"

"I'm learning, Mother!" Carrie grinned.

Then RoseMarie added, "Well, with that big wooden dough bowl always setting there with the flour ready, and the lard setting there ready to dip out a handful, it takes only a minute or so to mix up a batch of pie dough and then roll it out. So, I don't think you need to worry, Billy."

The six of them were soon settled at their places with the amiable family warmth around them making that food even more tempting. And after Ethan's words of thanks for their many blessings, those ample dishes began to be passed around.

Everyone, not only Ethan, loved these evenings. The busyness of the day accomplished and behind them, the appetizing aroma filling the room, the tone was set for light-hearted family camaraderie.

As Billy placed a mound of the mashed potatoes on his plate beside a nicely browned chicken thigh along with a leg, he used the serving spoon to press down the middle. Making a hollow, he waited for the gravy to be passed. And he commented to one of the hired men, "Pete, when you and Alvie were handling all those potatoes today, I'll bet you never even gave it a thought that they'd ever be looking this good, did you?"

"No sir, Billy, I sure didn't. In fact, they jest looked like a purtty big dirty job that had to be done! I shoulda treated 'em more special, right?"

Then Ethan said, "Well, tell us, Billy. Did you have any trouble getting the folks' tickets over at the station?"

"Nope, we got that all done and got them settled in their seat without a hitch," Billy answered. "You know, this morning I thought they acted like they were kind of dragging their feet, like they dreaded to go. But, then, as we got closer to Danville, they began to act more like they were looking forward to it."

Concerned for them, RoseMarie spoke up, "Well that's a long trek to be taking clear to Cincinnati, Ohio. It very well can be dangerous. Those two are getting pretty old to be going on such a venture."

Billy replied, "That could have been part of their trouble. But they talked a lot about how much they liked it here, saying this is such a beautiful place."

Carrie broke in to say, "But, then, like Billy said, by the time we neared Danville, they were beginning to talk about getting back to their own home again. They were imagining that the younger ones would have grown so much they probably wouldn't know them. And Grandfather sounded anxious to see how the boys were doing in the mill."

Remembering that touching farewell, Billy shared, "We got their baggage taken care of and they were all ready to board the train. Caleb was shaking my hand, and he said, 'Billy, after we're home awhile, I'd like to come back for another stay.' And, the way he said it, I know he really meant it!"

"Of course he meant it," Ethan smiled. "When he was telling me 'goodbye' here this morning he said the same thing to me."

All around the table, it was agreed that would be a nice thing to happen. Ethan remarked, "It's nice to have the wise head of an older experienced person to assure you in important undertakings. And the older I get, the more I know this for a fact."

Quietly, those younger ones thought on that for a moment.

As they talked, Billy's coffee cup was gradually filling with bread crusts.

Watching Billy carefully pulling off a crust, Alvie began to chuckle aloud. He said, "Miz B, this bread ya baked sure's good, but don'tcha think it'd be a good idea for us to make a fire outside again and let'cha make an oven full of them biskits out there? I kinda miss 'em!"

A ripple of good laughter passed around the table.

Pete asked, "Ethan, where didja git all these new-fangled ideas that ya had built into this house and the other buildin's anyhow?"

Billy jumped in with an answer to that, "Would you believe he gets his ideas by sitting around watching bonfires burning, Pete? He says it makes him dream! Isn't that right, Ethan?"

"Yes, Billy." Ethan said. "I did tell you about that. I do like to sit and watch a little fire burn, and the dreams just seem to take place. I get to thinking about things. Like how I used to watch my folks work and I could always see how they needed a bigger place. Then when Rosie and I got married, I'd watch her at work. And I began to see ways of how things could be made simpler and easier."

Drinking his coffee, taking bites of that good pie, he went on, "I think it's a fact that every generation will always have life easier than the one before. I never got to see my grandparents. They were always so far away, back in Pennsylvania. But listening to my father and mother tell about their own early childhood, I know my folks' new life in Ohio was easier and better than that of their parents."

Ethan was quiet a moment, musing, then he said, "During those long, awful war days all we could do was work long hard hours and try to keep up our end. Then, thinking about a place like this began to look possible. And I guess things just sorta happened."

He grinned at the ones around him. "We sure had things humming there for a while, didn't we?"

Each shook his head, smiling and agreeing.

Billy spoke up, "Ethan, there's one thing here that still seems unfinished. I've never heard you talk about it, but it's those pine trees out there in the corner of the front yard. I've never asked you why you set them out in a circle like you did. Why did you do them that way, Ethan? And then just leave them?"

Ethan grinned, "Well, Billy, I 've not said anything yet because I'm still working on my plan for that circle of pines.

It's still just tossing around in my mind. For one thing, I have to wait for them to get a little taller. And then, I'm going to turn that little circle into a screened-in room!"

"A what?" those five people all exclaimed at once.

Then Billy asked, "Alright, Ethan, go on. Tell us about it. Just what is a screened-in room?"

"Well, maybe you haven't noticed, but that circle is about right for a good-sized room. I'm going to make a frame to fit inside that circle and cover it in screen wire like's on our window screens. I'm still working on that plan. I know I'll have to allow for the trees to keep growing. And I'll make a screen door for it on this side toward the house."

Ethan had begun to show some of his old excitement, just like before, whenever he talked about details of plans. He could see his audience was pondering over what he was telling them. He said, "Can't you just picture us sitting out there in summertime, all comfortable, no bugs, no flies? Maybe even eating a meal out there? When dark comes we can use a lantern or two to light it up." He was wanting them to be excited about it too.

Then he said, "When those trees get to be a summer or two bigger, then we'll screen in that circle. I can't wait to sit out there of an evening, listening to the breeze blowing through the pine tops. It makes a soft, swooshing sound, almost like a whispering. I love to hear that. In fact, I've been thinking… I want to make that the name of this place, 'Whispering Pines'!"

RoseMarie was outwardly touched. Ever so softly she said, "Oh, Ethan! That's so beautiful. 'Whispering Pines.' I love that."

And Carrie said, "Papa, I want to live here forever! Let's start calling it that right now!" Ethan was just sure he could see tears in his daughter's eyes.

The rest of the evening was spent in the usual way, the women cleaning up the kitchen, putting food away, and winding things down for the night. They joined the men, then, in the next room where they had gone to sit in more comfortable chairs to read or talk.

This was the large dining room with its table that was used for eating when "company" came. Otherwise the family used the room for evening lounging or sometimes they played games around the table. It seemed cozier than the adjoining living room and certainly more so than the parlor that opened through wide French-type doors at the back end of the living room. That parlor was strictly for entertaining special company!

Sometimes on a cool evening, if it wasn't too dark and if the mosquitoes weren't too bad, they'd step out onto the roofed-over porch. Sitting there, they could look out toward the yard gate down at the road. And looking down the yard to the left of the porch, Ethan could see his circle of pines.

The big ornate Seth Thomas clock, setting there on its wall shelf, chimed out nine gongs in melodious style. Alvie, with Pete agreeing, was the first to declare that it was bedtime. Those two said their "good nights," mentioning how dawn had a way of showing up pretty early some mornings.

Pete picked up the lighted coal oil lamp setting on the small table near him and the two men walked out into the kitchen.

Then with Pete going ahead to light the way, they went out into the little vestibule separating the ell of the kitchen and the outside back door. Here, while Pete held the lamp, Alvie, taking a match from his pocket, lighted one of the lanterns setting under the bench at the one end of the vestibule.

Pete took the lamp back into the kitchen, blowing out the flame and then setting it down. It would be needed there in the morning.

Setting the lantern on the floor then, the men went out into the darkness to take care of last-of-day urinary functions. On hearing them, Buddy came running to check out the commotion. The men took time to look at the stars. They could recognize some of them like the North Star with the big dipper and the little dipper. And they could see Orion.

Back in the little anteroom, across from the bench with the coat rack hooks on the board above it, was the stairway leading up to the "hired-hand bedroom" at the second floor level.

Picking up the lantern for lighting their way, Pete opened that door and the men went up to their beds.

This stairway was built in the space between the kitchen pantry room and the outside wall of the house. That bedroom did not connect with the other upstairs bedrooms in the front part of the house.

From it, though, was a door that opened to expose another stairway leading up to a huge attic room, creating a third story of the house. The floor of that attic was finished with foot-wide boards. It made a good place for storing fruits and vegetables through the bitter cold winters.

The potatoes from today's digging were now laid out on floor racks there, joining the onions and the carrots that had been packed in wooden boxes of dry dirt for better keeping.

Soon there would be several barrels of apples picked from certain "keeping apple" trees in the orchard. Winesaps and Romes would be among those.

The women always made several trips up and down those back stairs tending to keeping the men's beds made up or periodically changing the bedding, as well as for going to the attic for supplies.

Now with Pete and Alvie getting settled in their beds, Alvie said, "You know what I'm thinking, Pete?"

"Well now, Alvie, that's hard to tell." And Pete chuckled.

"Well, the way I'm thinking, you and me've got it purtty good here. We're gittin' good money for workin' and with the good board we oughta start stashin' our money away. Maybe we could git a little set-up of our own....like maybe git a start of hogs er maybe some cows. What d'ya think, Pete?"

"Well Alvie, look 't what dreamin's done for Ethan! I reckon you 'n me could do a little of it ourselves."

Most likely those two men went to sleep while giving that some tossing around. Never before had their young minds considered such a possibility.

After helping to tidy up the dining room, Billy and Carrie went up the front stairs to their bedroom. Their room was one of several on that part of the second floor.

Undressing, blowing out the lamp, Carrie and Billy climbed into their bed. Billy cuddled up to his wife. They could feel that breeze coming in the open windows gently billowing the curtains, normally a pleasant inducement for sleep.

But tonight with Ethan's plan of his screen-room in the pines bouncing about in their minds, the two were full of talk.

"Billy," Carrie commented, "Do you realize that this baby of ours is going to get to grow up in a regular wonderland? Compared with how you and I started out in our childhood, this baby is going to be living in a completely different and wonderful world! I can't begin to imagine this child's future!"

"I know, Carrie," and Billy hugged her gently. Then, playfully, he suggested, "With all these advantages, let's fill these rooms with babies!"

"Oh now, wait a minute. Billy, you're scaring me!" Then in the darkness and grinning happily, softly she said, "Well, let's do it one at a time!"

Ethan and RoseMarie were the last to retire. It was up to them to see that the flames in any of the lamps were not left burning.

Standing near the end of the table, Ethan reached upward to gently steady the specially built little basket-like frame that was holding a very pretty, ornate lamp. Carefully he tipped it enough to allow him to blow out the flame. He couldn't help but feel a bit of smug pride about this creation.

This overhead lighting was the culmination of one of his wild ideas.

To him it had always seemed that a lamp was never in the right place of a room. So when the ceiling of this dining room was being built, he'd seen to the installation of this whimsical addition.

Anchored into the ceiling about midway of the room over where the table would set, he'd installed a 6-foot long iron rod, extending it a couple of inches below and running out parallel to the ceiling. Then he rigged that ceiling anchor to allow the rod to be hand-rotated.

At the end, the 6-foot rod bent upward enough to form a little hook, and he'd had a decorative basket-like frame made, suspending it by a chain from that hooked end. The little hook kept the chain from sliding off. And nestled within the basket frame, a kerosene lamp could set there safely.

By taking hold of the basket frame, pulling it around, the lighted lamp could be swung around the room, stopping it at any desired point within its 12-foot diameter circle.

Even now, tonight, as he was handling it, Ethan was smiling, remembering. What a harassing time he'd had, trying to make the blacksmith understand what he wanted and then getting him to comply with Ethan's explanations.

The smithy said he didn't have time for such tomfoolery, that he had important things to make. But once he calmed down and listened and learned what Ethan would pay him for the job, his interest accelerated. Afterwards, the smithy was known to brag about his finished piece of work.

But now, utilizing this ingenious lighting system each evening, Ethan knew it was worth every one of those trying moments.

As he continued with his winding down for the night, Ethan left a couple of the doors and windows open to let in the breeze. At this time of year, with the cool night air still needed for comfort, the screen doors would keep out bugs or animals.

Ethan carried the last remaining lighted lamp with them as he and RoseMarie went into their downstairs bedroom.

That room opened off one side of the little hallway between the dining and living rooms. And just opposite their bedroom door was the door leading to the stairway down to the cellar.

Setting the lamp on the dresser, Ethan could hear Buddy outside the opened window. He knew the dog was getting settled on the back veranda.

All evening Buddy had been going from porch to porch to be near each arena of family commotion. Now in the darkness of night, all this became his domain.

Being well fed and having known only treatment of love and respect, Buddy exuded a contentment stemming out from family trust. That sleek, longhaired, brown and white collie dog felt a fierce loyalty and a need to protect. Tonight he would sleep, but as always, his innate subconscienceness would be alert, ready to guard and take command.

Coming through those screened open windows from the black darkness outside was the pleasant blend of night noises. It was easy to distinguish the noisy katydids over the screech owls calling back and forth. And into that natural harmony the smaller insects were making their presence known.

Blowing out the flame of that last lamp, Ethan was a smiling, contented man. His mind was already forming his prayer of good night.

Here he was, standing in the midst of the accomplishments of his dreams of yesterday. And today, his beloved parents' leaving for their own home back in the Ohio forest glen was like putting a stamp of "finished approval" on the whole project.

Now, there was tomorrow! With his voicing out loud the plan for the screen room in the circle of pines, it became a viable certainty.

With Buddy in charge, each family member could sleep peacefully. Each was confident knowing in the event of any disturbance, that faithful collie dog would be barking out a resounding alert.

SEVENTEEN

Mollie's Whispering Pines - 2002

"There's just something different about the feel of this day," Mollie was talking out loud to herself. Or, maybe to her dog, Sammie, stretched out there beside her. He was half sleeping, but with one eye following her movements as well as not missing anything else that might be going on.

She took a couple of sips of the hot coffee from the mug in her hand, and again out loud, *"Yes sir, I can just tell. Everything today is going to be okay!"* As she said the words her critical eyes made a sweep across the patio area there at the side door of the huge old farmhouse kitchen.

Mollie was anticipating company and at her age now it takes longer to get things into "company shape." But she still loved to do it. She never tired of sharing her beloved Whispering Pines. And company always seemed to love coming.

This company coming today, though, was different. It was her niece, Gail, with her family from Omaha, Nebraska. Gail was the granddaughter of Mollie's oldest brother. And Mollie had chosen Gail out of the whole big clan of the Ethan Bennett descendants to be the one to be handed down that old family treasure; a treasure dating way back to the mid 1800s.

She'd chosen Gail even though she'd not seen the girl since that one time she'd come on a visit. Gail must have been five or six years old at that time and had come with her folks and her grandparents. Now she was married with a husband and two big kids of her own.

But Mollie felt sure that she'd made the right choice. Throughout her long life she'd gotten pretty good at going with her gut feelings.

This family treasure, in the beginning back there in the mid 1800s, was a kitchen table. Mollie's old family ancestor, Ethan

Bennett, had made the table by hand. He'd cut down an oak tree growing in the forest on the Bennett homestead of that day where they lived along the river over in Ohio.

As the years had passed, Ethan and his own little family had come here to Illinois to build and settle on this farmland that he'd homesteaded in 1866.

He'd put up this building complex that had become the show place of the country; this place that he'd named Whispering Pines.

This little kitchen table, being special, had been amongst the few family belongings they'd brought from Ohio.

Coming first by riverboat on the Ohio, they'd docked and unloaded. Then they'd made the rest of the trip by horse-pulled wagons, coming north up the old Illinois Lincoln Trail to this tract of land where he'd built this farmstead.

From long use, the table had gotten old and broken. But for sentimental reasons it had been kept, laying around in one of the sheds.

Years later, Mollie's mother, knowing the history behind the table, had recognized the beauty still present in the wood. She had retrieved the useable parts of it, having them made into three candlesticks. Those candlesticks from that wood, so richly and elegantly lovely, reeked of heritage. And Mollie had acquired them along with the rest of Whispering Pines.

But of late she was becoming sensitive to logic. Especially concerning the fact that she herself was ever nearing the point of becoming an "estate." She felt that a caring younger descendant of the long extended line of the Bennett family needed to possess and care for those candlesticks.

After all, so blessed and so fortunate as she was, Mollie had already out-lived her relative peers. Her own kids had begun to mention the few years left until her big 100th birthday party! And while all that was exciting, she knew she needed to get busy at attending to important details.

So, after some long and careful deliberation, Gail had been the one she'd chosen. Even over her own kids. And she had UPS-ed them along with an explanatory note to Gail in Nebraska a few weeks earlier.

Now, this afternoon, taking this last look around, Mollie was satisfied in her inspection. Sitting down in one of the padded lawn chairs, she settled back, shifting herself to get comfortable. *"Ooh, but I do feel so good,"* again she was talking to herself out loud. Sammie moved his tail a bit as if to lazily wag it in happy agreement.

Mollie had earned this good feeling. Knowing for a while that those kids would be arriving today, along with her many naps needed for body reparation, she had worked hard to get things in readiness. Now she was all green-for-go and ready to have fun with these kids!

Taking another sip of coffee, she smiled contentedly, thinking, *"even this coffee tastes better than usual…I got a good 'scald' on it, that's for sure."* Mollie owed that little fun sentiment to her dad from his growing up days, way back long, long ago.

Back then at hog butchering time for the winter's meat, all the necessary gear would be in readiness out there in the barn lot. In readiness for a very hard, busy, but productive day.

A neighbor or so with all of the family would have come to help which meant, along with their help, even the kitchen would become a beehive of preparation as well. Come noontime, a veritable feast had to be ready for satisfying all those many appetites. Appetites that were whetted even more so by the jolliness of the atmosphere when friends gather together.

An important step in preparation included the water boiling in the huge iron vat, the fire burning under it there in the barnyard, all ready for the quick dousing of the freshly-killed hog carcass. Getting a "good scald" would ensure a clean "scraping off" of the hog hair…and that was a most helpful bonus in good butchering! A good scald and clean scraping ensured good smooth bacon rinds, many of which became those excellent "cracklins" when the fat was baked out of them!

Even Mother Nature was performing at her best in this June scene, as if she herself was happy in helping Mollie set this stage of pleasantry. The mid-afternoon sun was warm and inviting. The pink and the white periwinkles bordering the patio, sporting their pretty colors, were doing their part in enhancing the whole panorama.

Mollie was ready. And those Nebraska kids should be arriving any minute now.

Relaxing, sipping at her coffee, Mollie's mind began to slow. Like the periwinkles, she too was enhancing this scene… unaware, of course. Sporting her pretty silver-white hairdo, accented by the colorful shorts and top set that she'd chosen to wear; she was a part of that pretty picture.

With her free hand, she smoothed out her shorts. Mollie always felt good in her shorts. She remembered living through those early olden times when women and girls had to clad themselves in restrictive feminine clothes.

When still a young girl, it was always a dress and above-the-knee length cotton hose, most often ugly black. All those petticoats, camisoles, bloomers, and that awful long-legged, long-sleeved underwear was for tolerating the cold winters. Although, back in those olden days that long underwear felt good. It was accepted as a blessing. With no heat in the upstairs bedrooms of those middle class homes, staying warm at night had to be dealt with. Or when walking that nearly a mile to school in deep snow.

She smiled to herself now, lazily letting out a little sigh and shaking her head. Thank goodness for the ease she enjoyed in handling today's clothing. Such changes she'd lived through since those old times of her early school years.

How could she ever forget those winter morning procedures of getting those hose put on wrinkle free over those long underwear legs. There was a knack to doing that. And to master that knack took patience and some practice!

Mollie could remember how she would roll up an underwear leg to above her knee. Then she'd put on a long stocking, pulling it up to its full length above her knee, then carefully roll it back down to her ankle. Next, she'd unroll the underwear back down to her ankle. Lapping it at the ankle to make a tight fit, she'd hold that lapped underwear leg carefully while beginning to unroll the stocking back up over it, ending with it above her knee again. Then she'd secure her stocking with an elastic garter. And then she'd do the other leg.

Today all that seems so involved, but in those days, of course, it was just routine. Either the winters back then were colder or the olden means of combating the cold were too inadequate.

Again Mollie smiled thinking about it. That old underwear was soft and warm. Clean ones were put on after each weekly Saturday bath, and barring accidents, were not removed until the following Saturday. With the washing of clothes back then done manually in a wash tub with rubbing on a washboard for removing heavy soil, "wash day" was day-long and hard work.

And during the long winters when temperatures were at freezing levels, getting the clothes dried was equally laborsome. Lengths of rope as clothesline would be strung across a room, generally the big kitchen, with the heat from the stove serving as the drying source.

Mollie smiled to herself, dredging up those old memories. Of one thing, she mused; dehydration of the family members was never a problem! They were almost never sick back in those days.

She also recalled the verbal admonishment concerning having respect for her clothing.

What a relief as gradual liberation progressed. Especially, finally, when simple carefree shorts became acceptable as casual dress.

Now, Mollie's closet contained numerous shorts sets. It was her preferred choice of clothing whenever the weather barely hinted of warmth. Even when that hint was only half reliable, she just put on a sweatshirt, still donning those shorts.

Mollie's philosophy had long been, whenever company was coming, to get things all clean and pretty in readiness for them, and then the minute that company arrived, go "on vacation" with them. Enjoy them; enjoy yourself!

So now she was ready. She was getting anxious to have this little vacation begin!

She'd always made it a point to stay in touch with her relatives. And of those there were many. With her being one of several siblings, there were numerous nieces and nephews plus grandchildren and great-grandchildren through her own kids. But, with Mollie's longevity now, she'd been there when far too many of the older clan had been laid to rest.

During family get-togethers, whether on somber occasions or happy events, she found it so refreshing to be around the young people. It fed her vibrancy, learning of the ways of today, then incorporating anything useful into her own lifestyle.

Now, over the last several days, she'd been busily preparing for this day's occasion and Mollie's almost 86-year old bones where showing rebellion...in spite of the many interspersing naps. She appreciated this quiet time now. It would allow for what she termed as a time for some "body repair!"

At any moment now, driving through that barn lot gate, would be her great niece, Gail Hinton. And there would be Gail's husband, Bruce, and their two kids, Holy Rose and Ethan. Strangers, they were driving from their home in Bellevue, Nebraska, adjacent to Omaha.

Resting, relishing this interlude, Mollie gazed out across the area before her. Her beloved "Whispering Pines." That was the name given this farm many, many years ago by that first Ethan...the pioneer grandfather...'way back almost a century and a half ago.

For Mollie that very name, Whispering Pines, had ever emitted a feeling of peacefulness. And with it there was always a feeling of such a solid stability.

She was born into this. Born right here in this house, years before, in 1916, as had her mother long years before that. But during these last years, with the normal process of change and aging, the farmstead's building complex itself had taken on a general appearance of neglect. The entire complex was run down, out dated. The few buildings that were still standing were no longer useful in this fast-paced technical world of today with its new methods of agriculture.

And, Mollie…pretty as she felt and refreshing as she looked…was well aware of reality; aware that she, in actuality, blended right into this tapestry of antiquity.

But this same aura of stability and peacefulness exuded from Mollie herself, an aura that had settled in and around her as she had lived and learned through her own normal process of aging. Mollie WAS Whispering Pines. That came as part of her birth, right in this big ol' house.

Now, sipping her mid-afternoon coffee, momentarily quiet and more rested as she was becoming, she was beginning to tingle with excitement. After all, she had made that important decision. She had chosen this great-niece, Gail Hinton, to be the recipient of those old wooden candlesticks, treasured heirlooms as they were. It was a choice she had made after a great deal of consideration.

Gail was a granddaughter of one of Mollie's older brothers, a brother who had died several years ago. This was a niece she'd met only once and that was when the girl was very young. Mollie knew of her mostly through the family genealogy and through family letters, although those of late had been quite intermittent. But now, today, the girl would be coming.

When Gail had phoned saying she'd gotten the package, Mollie was so pleased when the girl showed such interest in wanting to learn more of the family's background. Mollie felt sure she'd chosen the right descendant to carry on with this family treasure.

Over the phone Gail had said that in studying the map, it seemed their best bet would be to get a motel in Hooperston and drive out to the farm from there. But Mollie had convinced her that they would be missing a valuable firsthand experience in this part of the family tree by not staying right out here at the farm.

Mollie just knew that young Ethan Hinton needed to have some time walking the very ground that the former Ethan had walked. She wanted these young people to get the feel of this tangible family connection. She wanted to help them trod back in time and explore this portion of their legacy.

Mollie was a firm believer that things like that build solidity of character. Plus she was quite adamant in her belief that certain family descendants should be entrusted with important family heirlooms. With her being so filled to the brim with the history of happenings over her long lifetime in conjunction with this place, her Whispering Pines, she was ever eager to share her sentiments and her knowledge of this part of the family lore.

Too, besides all that serious stuff, Mollie loved having company and she had plenty of room.

EIGHTEEN

The Vacation in Illinois

"There it is, Bruce, there's the Gilbert Street exit just like Aunt Mollie's map says!" Excitedly Gail pointed to the interstate overhead sign.

They'd been approaching Danville, Illinois, on East I-74 having passed through Champaign-Urbana, the home of the University of Illinois, about 40 miles back. All this was strange territory to this young family, although, really the trip so far had been a snap.

Just as she had promised, Aunt Mollie had mailed them a directive map, a detailed computer printout. And this map was something else! Beginning with the kid's own street address in Bellevue, Nebraska, every little detailed bit of their trip coverage was clearly and precisely printed out. It included lengths of mileage straightway to Mollie's country gate.

Bruce had insisted they would take two days in making this trip and Gail had agreed. She felt lucky in that he'd agreed to make the trip at all. Up to now, their short vacations had been spent pretty much close to home.

After eating their breakfast yesterday morning, they'd left their home near Omaha. With Gail as the family navigator, she had kept that map handy.

In Omaha they'd picked up I-80 East, crossing the Missouri River into Iowa, coming on east to the Mississippi nearing Davenport where they'd picked up I-74. After crossing the Illinois River at Peoria, Illinois, they'd found the Holiday Inn Express motel where Gail had pre-arranged for reservations.

There they'd gotten settled in for the fun evening. The four of them had enjoyed the motel swimming pool and the kids had explored the arcade games. Now today, they expected an easy drive on to Danville and then on out to Mollie's country place.

As Bruce exited off onto Danville's Gilbert Street, Gail expressed pleased gratitude on having such a detailed map. Looking over at Bruce, she remarked, "You know, honey, I can't wait to meet this Mollie person. I know she's old and I know what old people look like. But she throws me off with things she said over the phone. And now with this fantastic travel thing! We can't do this with our computer, can we?"

Bruce, adjusting with the Gilbert Street traffic, sort of grumbled, "No, that's a software I've never felt we needed."

He was still about half-miffed that they were even coming on this inane goose chase. Even more so that Gail had agreed to their staying out there in the boondocks at that farmhouse instead of getting a motel in one of the towns. What a waste of vacation days.

"Hey Dad, I'm starving," eleven year old Ethan stated from the back seat.

And Holly agreed saying, "It is noontime, Dad." Then, "Oh, hey, look…there's a Ponderosa just ahead!"

"Okay gang. I guess a pit stop will do us good." Coming to the restaurant, Bruce maneuvered into a parking spot. Getting out of their SUV, it was nice to stretch and walk a bit.

Back on the roadway, they as well as the gas tank sated, Bruce noted that Gilbert Street was also Rt. 1, and that was what they wanted.

Soon they were out of the city and heading on north. Within a few miles a town called Rossville appeared and Mollie's map showed a turn off into the country with only a few miles on to the farmstead....their destination. And it was still early afternoon.

Wending along those country roads, Bruce was saying, "Today is June 10th, 2002. A month ago who would have ever thought that I'd be out here in this God-forsaken place?" Everybody just smiled. Even the car just purred along.

The kids were relieved that the trip was about over, not giving a whole lot of thought as to what lay ahead. Bruce knew exactly what lay ahead...boredom and a complete waste of good time.

Gail, on the other hand, sensed excitement, looking forward to meeting this aunt. Since her surprise in receiving those beautiful candlesticks with Aunt Mollie's note arousing her intrigue, she wanted to know more. Gail was looking forward to learning more about her family's early history.

NINETEEN

Trodding Back in Time

Sitting out there on the patio with the warm sun enveloping her, Mollie was all relaxed and so comfortable. She was about half asleep when Sammie sprang to his feet, giving a sharp bark. Noting the car slowing at the gateway of the barn lot, she said, "Quiet, Sammie, it's all right."

Momentarily, coming to a stop, the car hesitated then turned in through the open gateway. It was a late model SUV. Slowly it pulled up by the small gate in the fence separating the barn lot and the yard. Stopping, the engine was turned off.

Mollie stood up…wide-awake. The car doors opened. Everybody began to get out, stretching and looking around.

Suddenly, that quiet summer afternoon was jolted into a surprised reaction…young Ethan had let out a yell! He was hollering, "Mom, Dad, look! It's a stile!" and quick as a flash he was up those two steps and standing on the top of the old stile, there in the fence line abutting the closed yard gate.

In disbelief, Ethan continued to holler, "This is exactly like the one in the picture of my old Mother Goose book, remember?" He was so excited. "Remember the story you used to read to me? About when the old woman found a penny and went to the market and bought a pig? But going home they came to the stile and the pig wouldn't go over it! And the old woman said 'The pig won't go over the stile and I shan't get home tonight!' You remember…" He stopped to catch his breath, and then he walked down the two steps on the other side.

Holly, caught up in her brother's excitement, was soon right behind him, trailing him down the two steps on the other side and into the yard.

Mollie, up on the patio a hundred or so feet away, was laughing. Bruce and Gail, still standing by the car, were laughing. Then, opening the little gate, they walked through, turning, with Bruce closing and latching it behind them. What a moment!

Any "iciness" between strangers had thawed instantly!

At a glance, Mollie saw a dad and a mom, each probably nearing forty, healthy and good looking, the dad with light brown hair and his face clean-shaven, while the mom was a pretty brunette. And Mollie saw a young boy and a girl....probably a couple of years older....who were equally healthy and good looking and ready for some action.

In that same exchange of glances, Bruce and Gail saw a lady standing there on her patio, all smiles, looking eager and inviting and anything but "old!"

Bruce just couldn't help himself...a spark of expectation was lighting up even within him!

And the kids, with their wide-sweeping glance taking in that huge shaded yard with its many paths leading to that big old 3-story house, just stood there in awe. They just knew they had plunged into the courtyard of an old castle.

Introductions out of the way, Mollie was admonishing them to "make themselves right at home with no formalities." Inviting them to sit a moment on the patio, she asked if they would like something cold to drink, or for the grownups, perhaps some hot coffee.

But first, young Ethan needed to use the bathroom.

Grinning, Mollie said, "Bruce, let's break Ethan in right off the bat. Take him around the house, then down the path, and let him use the outhouse. Probably he's never been in one of those in his whole life."

Well, for that matter, neither had Bruce! So, smiling and chattering, the two of them took off around the house. Mollie took Gail and Holly inside where they could use the regular bathroom, and now they were back out on the patio. Mollie had brought out a tray with glasses of ice cubes and some cans of sodas. Gail was already sitting comfortably, enjoying a mug of refreshing hot coffee.

Bruce and Ethan soon returned to join them. Ethan was bubbling with that newfound discovery...that outhouse, "Mom, he said excitedly, "That place is so cool! You open the door and there's a sort of bench-like seat with two holes in it. You just go to the toilet down one of the holes...honest. It just goes down on the ground underneath...and you don't flush it! There's regular toilet paper, but there's a big old Sears and Roebuck catalogue hanging on a hook. Dad said that's what people used to use for toilet paper...he said he'd read about that." Ethan was talking so fast he was out of breath.

Laughing, Bruce opened a can of soda pouring it over the ice cubes in one of the glasses and then he settled himself into one of the patio chairs. Ethan opted to do the same.

"Aunt Mollie," Gail began, "That map you sent us was a Godsend. Did you do that yourself? How did you know where to begin it...and where to send it? For that matter how did you even know that we existed?"

Mollie grinned at Gail. "Well now kids, thanks to our tremendous technical appliances, getting the answers to what you're asking with my computer software is a piece of cake. Then, Gail, you're grandfather was my brother. We grew up in this house together. And when all of us married and scattered we stayed in touch with each other. I still have my invitation to your wedding. I don't remember why but there was some reason that Tom and I couldn't go."

Already Mollie was liking these kids and she could sense their interest.

She went on. "What clinched our getting together with your getting those candlesticks was through you, Holly Rose!" Mollie looked at the young girl, smiling. Holly had been sipping her drink, listening, but now she looked surprised!

"How ever did I have anything to do with all this?" she asked.

"About a couple of months ago I was casually reading my Danville Commercial News and there was the article about an essay written by a Holly Rose Hinton from Bellevue, Nebraska." Holly was all ears!

"The paper said that your essay, Holly, was the 1st place winner in a contest on 'What It Can Mean To Be a Teenager in 2002.' The caption stated that you were a freshman at Bellevue East High School. It said that the contest was statewide and the 1st place award was a $1,000 US savings bond."

The expression on Mollie's face was one of pride. She went on, "You better believe I read every word of that essay. Holly, I was so impressed!"

Looking fondly at the pretty young girl, she added, "The editor of our Illinois newspaper had to be impressed as well, even to run the story on it and print the essay."

Pausing thoughtfully, Mollie said, "You see, I knew of your mom and dad through your great-grandfather...and your grandmother in California, and I have kept in touch now and then. She'd written me when you were born, Holly. You too, Ethan. So, I've always known *'of'* you. Then when I ready your essay, knowing it was a very part of you, I also knew a lot *'about'* you!"

Mollie smiled at Holly, going on, "Just reading those things you'd written even went a long way in telling me about what kind of parents you've had to have reared the girl who could write those things!"

It was Holly's turn to be impressed. She said, "Well, gosh, Aunt Mollie, thank you. I'd never have guessed that any little words of mine would ever reach out this far!"

"Uh-huh, that's true. We never know who may be watching or listening. Back to your essay, you said some pretty wise things, my dear."

"Thank you. Well, it was a pretty challenging subject. I gave it a lot of thought; about this crazy world we kids have to live in. You know, it's really hard to be a teenager. But you don't become one just overnight…well, in age you do, but you don't make a visible change overnight. Then, I remembered something my mom said about all those little cubicles in her workplace. How each worker is expected to produce when confined to such a tiny space. But Mom said 'it's what you as an individual take into that space with you that makes the difference!' And I thought that's it! It's the same with us teenagers."

Holly paused, glancing at her parents. Then she went on, "What we've learned from things we've been taught and how we've acted during the leading up to this time is what we take into it. And just like Mom said, I think that makes all the difference. With good discipline and training along with good examples to prepare us, that helps us to think sensibly about today's opportunities. And one thing is for sure, there's no shortage today in opportunities." Mollie could feel the pride exuding from Bruce and Gail.

Even young Ethan seemed to be taking in what his sister was saying.

Mollie said, "Well, Holly, as I said, I liked what I read. And for me, all those little unspoken family values that oozed out of your words made me look on you and your family with a lot of respect."

Holly felt so encouraged as she listened to what this woman was saying. It was nice to know they were related. And she wanted to add this one more thing. She'd mentioned something about it in her article also. "You know, I have this best friend, Meredith, and we talk over everything. We always feel so badly when we hear of some kid like us who, in a moment of pure stupidity, does something that ruins his life forever. In the flash of one little instant, poof, the doors to his opportunities are closed! What a waste." Holly even looked sad as she spoke.

Mollie said, "Well, Holly, that doesn't stop with teenagers. That goes right on with people of all ages, sorry to say," and Bruce and Gail nodded in agreement.

For a moment it was quiet on the patio. Then Mollie, smiling at the little family, said, "When I read that essay, that was when I knew you guys should be the ones to take charge of those heirlooms, those old candlesticks! Also, I haven't told you this, but I have the journals that Ethan Bennett's sister Carrie wrote all those long years ago. They're written on old parchment paper." Mollie was excited, talking about it.

She continued, "Those yellowed papers date back to the early 1820s. They're old family history stuff…Carrie Bennett wrote those first ones using a feather quill pen that she had to keep dipping in an inkbottle. Then Ethan's own daughter, also named Carrie after her aunt, kept up an on-going log. And one generation after another has kept that tradition going."

Pausing a moment, looking at the kids, she said, "Do you realize what a treasure those writings are? How special they are for our big family today?"

Mollie had to chuckle then. She said, "You know, it's interesting in those writings, how the type of pens they had to use kept changing. First it was those long used old feather quills with the one end of the feather shaft cut on a slant to make a sharpened point. It had to be dipped often into that inkbottle!" Mollie was remembering about this first hand!

She went on, "Next a type of metal pen point was invented. The pen point was inserted into the end of a pencil-shaped holder. But even those pens still had to be dipped often into an inkbottle. Now those were the same kind of pen that I used in my early school days in the old 8-grade, one room schoolhouse! Each school desk's slanted top had a little round hole cut in the upper right hand corner for an inkbottle to set. Inkbottles were styled to fit those holes. Gosh, how I remember those old pens. In fact, I have a few of them yet. Those pen points were always getting bent, or the split ends of the point always getting spread apart from pressure. And inkbottles were always getting upset. What a mess. During writing, we had absorbent paper blotters to use. Those blotters were very necessary in blotting and drying the written words. When I was a kid business places gave away blotters with their advertising logo on one side. And we could buy different colors of ink, like black, blue, green or red. I even remember having violet ink." Mollie paused. She hadn't thought about these old ways of doing for a long time.

She continued then, "But I remember we kids mostly used pencils for writing. Schools always had pencil sharpeners mounted on a wall or on a corner of the teacher's big desk. There was a little hand-turned crank for operating it. At home we had to use a paring knife for whittling off the pencil wood and sharpening off the lead to make a point. Now, those were the days!"

Mollie laughed. "Then, thank goodness, came typewriters and fountain pens! Those pens were made with a little long barrel with a rubber insert that sucked up a fill of ink. Much like a turkey baster works today. And a fill of ink would last through a lot of writing before the next refill. Finally then came the wonderful ballpoints. And now your fantastic world of computers and e-mail!"

Everybody laughed. But those younger minds had grasped the amazement.

Ethan put a voice to his emotions, saying, "Cool!"

Mollie said, "That's a good way to put it, Ethan. It is definitely 'cool'." Then she added one more thing. "And I've already decided, no longer than I've known you, you young people are going to be the ones I'm going to entrust with these priceless old family history files. And with Xerox machines or fast print places like Kinko's, copies could be run off for any interested relatives."

She smiled at those kids. "I've always known it's a fact that life wouldn't go on forever here at this old sanctuary as it has through all these past generations. And when my husband, Tom, died, leaving me alone here, that fact became a closer reality. So it's bothered me some that I needed to be finding the right new homes for the special family relics."

Again she paused, then, "Tomorrow we'll get that old stuff out and you can look at it. You can decide if you would accept it and take it home with you."

With that Mollie got up, picking up her coffee mug. She said, "Even though I know I shouldn't be drinking this much coffee, I'm going in and get a refill". Noting that Gail had set her empty mug on the patio table, she asked, "How about you, Gail? Shall I bring out the pot?"

"Oh why not, it's so pleasant sitting here. And your coffee does taste so-o good," Gail answered, and she picked up a cookie as she spoke.

The plate of homemade cookies was setting on the patio table where Mollie had set it earlier. It was being protected from the insects with a specially made tent-like netted covering. Now and then a honeybee would be a part of that June atmosphere, busy with its gathering nectar from the brightly blooming flowers bordering the patio.

Returning, Mollie refilled Gail's mug and then her own. With the coffee pot nearly empty, she set it on the little table, then got comfortable again in her own chair.

Sipping now and then at his glass of soda, Bruce, thoughtfully, was taking in every bit of this. Having spent his life so far as a "city boy" he'd never yet experienced a country scene such as this. And the truth was he was enjoying it! He couldn't remember when he'd felt this kind of relaxation. Things here, out here in this big countryside space, were such a contrast to his Omaha area. It just wasn't…well, it wasn't so busy-like! And Gail's Aunt Mollie intrigued him. He'd never been around an old person like her.

Feeling full of questions he said, "Aunt Mollie…oh, may I call you 'Aunt Mollie'?"

She answered, "Of course, I want you to. Probably a hundred or so call me either 'Aunt' or 'Gram-ma' and I love it. I'm even a great-great gram-ma now! You know, getting to live to be nearly 86 years old, I'm just bound to have made a lot of history!"

Gail had to chime in at this point, "Aunt Mollie, I can't get over how good you look. I'd never believe you're that old. You look far better in those shorts than I do in mine."

Mollie smiled, "Now Gail…but, thank you. Well, I live in shorts from the earliest warm spring day to the last warm day of fall. Long ago, growing up, when shorts first came into being, I was taught that 'ladies do not wear shorts out in public,' so I didn't. But as custom changed and I could get by with them, shorts became my favorite clothing. And then with retirement age and with competition and limitations dropping off, look out! You know, when you get to that point, you can be a 'rebel!' I am one and I love it!"

Bruce had picked up a couple of the cookies and had sat back comfortably in his padded chair. He had been listening, waiting and now he said, "Okay you two, it's my turn for questions. Aunt Mollie, first I have to say this. I had my own opinion of what 'old ladies' look like! Do you know you've blown that opinion right out of the water?"

They all laughed at that.

Then Bruce asked, "Aunt Mollie, how come you've kept that old outhouse? I was surprised to see it so clean and still usable."

Mollie told him, "Well, that's for two reasons. First, it's handy when working outside. Illinois is known for its black soil and, after a rain or when there's dew on the grass of a morning, one's shoes get muddy and dirty. So it's very convenient to go into that one outside. Then secondly, it's an antique. We older people who grew up with that as our only means of a toilet get a kick out of having one around, making us appreciate the ones in the house. Inside plumbing that you young people take for granted is one of the many blessings that we older people count daily."

She smiled at Bruce, continuing, "And then, just like Ethan, the young visitors look on that outhouse as a novelty. It's an experience for them. So…I keep it scrubbed up, a throw rug on the floor, and periodically I sprinkle lime down inside it so it's acceptable, odorwise."

Listening thoughtfully Bruce said, "Honestly, I didn't know what to expect coming here as we have. And…again, honestly, I'm impressed. You do live here alone now?"

"Yes I do, Bruce. Just me and my reliable partner, Sammie. And I'm very comfortable. I'm going to hate giving it up. Tom was my good buddy, my wonderful mate, and when I lost him a few years ago, I wanted to remain here with all my beautiful memories. After all, my mother was born in this house long ago, back in 1889, and I was born here along with my siblings. And one of those siblings, of course, was your grandfather, Gail."

"My folks farmed the land as long as they could, like Ethan and the others following him. Then when Tom and I bought it from my parents, we farmed it until it was no longer prudent for us to do so. For one thing, we were getting older, and also it was no longer possible to make a decent living on only 160 acres of land. A big conglomerate 'business farmer' had been wanting to buy it, so we sold the place…but with one stipulation. We had a signed contract specifying that we could stay on here in this house and use the barn lot as long as we were alive or wanted to. So now I'm sure the bulldozers are more than ready to come in when I'm done with it. The yard and barn lot will no doubt become grain fields."

"Does that make you sad, Aunt Mollie?" Gail was quick to ask.

"No, not really. Not with the full busy life I've been privileged to have. Anyway this is the natural sequence of how aging is supposed to be. 'Stepping aside to progress' I believe it's called."

Taking a swig of coffee Mollie looked at Bruce, asking, "Did you know that it was in 1866 when Ethan Bennett came here from Ohio and homesteaded this land? The Civil War had just ended in 1865 when President Lincoln was assassinated. And Ethan and RoseMarie's young son, John, had been killed on his way back home from that war. I'm sure things were pretty crazy at that time."

"No, I didn't know that. Gail, you never knew about any of these things did you?"

Shaking her head she said, "No. My gosh! I've never heard my folks talk about it. But then, Bruce, since you and I've been married we've lived a long way from my parents."

Gail looked at her son who had been listening intently, drinking his cola. She said, "Just think, you and this other Ethan have the same name but with all these years in between you!" Young Ethan just grinned.

Mollie was saying, "This house and lay out was Ethan Bennett's dream come true! His mind just had to be filled with novel ideas for his day. This turned out to be the showplace of the country! And it's been passed down through family members all these many generations."

She paused a moment, thoughtfully, then said, "When I got married my older siblings were already out on their own and the two younger ones were still in school. My husband, Tom, had already been working for my parents as a farm hand, so we just stayed on, living here with them. And when they both had died and all their business affairs were settled, Tom and I had bought out the shares of the others and we just kept right on with the farming."

Mollie continued, "Actually all this has worked out fine for me. I'm sure you kids have noticed that everywhere you look the buildings, including the big house, are in a state of serious neglect. And one day, in all natural probability, some normal old age situation will flare up and I no longer can remain independent like I am now. I could have some freak accident and that could even be tomorrow. Or it can be years yet ahead. I'll face that when it happens. But it's sure comforting to read and hear about all the advances being made in the field of caring for the aged."

She smiled, shifting her position in her chair, saying, "Heck, maybe by the time when I might have to face something like that, there'll be such new and improved facilities that it may not be too bad."

Going on then, "But now when I look around this place, with everything so familiar, I don't even see the neglect. I just revel in all the old happiness I sense around me. And selling the land, having the money, as Tom and I did, we've been able to keep up the necessary repairs and improvements. Through the years we'd modernized where we could and where we thought we needed to. Even before Tom died we could visualize the picture of our future ahead of us. But it was never sad. We just looked at it as normal life. Happy people always adjust with the times. It's only the people who can't adjust who have no happiness!"

As Gail had listened to all this, quietly sipping at her coffee, taking bites of cookie, she'd been watching her old aunt as if studying her. Now, smiling she said, "Aunt Mollie, you amaze me! It's been such a long time since I was that little kid, coming here to visit you and Uncle Tom. Coming here with my folks and my grandparents. I don't remember too much about it but I do recall, though, that I had such a fun time. There was so much here to explore. I remember that even then you always were ready to show me everything. That whole memory has always felt good; all warm and pleasant." And for a brief moment that pleasure was reflected in Gail's pretty face.

That gave Mollie a good feeling also with her mind visualizing Gail as that little girl so long ago.

Bruce, too, was feeling good, so relaxed the way he was, listening.

Then Gail was saying, "But now, meeting you again like this, like strangers after all these years, you're not a bit like I thought you'd be. I expected you to be an old grandmotherly type woman. After all, I knew your age from my granddad's records. And, gosh Gram-pa's been gone for a long time now."

Gail stopped, looking at Mollie carefully, then trying to be tactful she said, "Now, Aunt Mollie, forgive me for saying this but logic tells me you've just had to have already lived the biggest bulk of your life!"

Gail paused thoughtfully showing fondness in her look at her aunt, then she went on, "But you look as though you're still right in the middle of things. You just can't be as old as the records say you are!" Laughing she added, "Boy, I sure hope I've inherited a big share of your genes!"

Mollie was smiling too, sensing that fondness permeating the little scene there on that comfortable patio. Even the June afternoon seemed to be affected, responding at its best.

Bruce, looking at his watch and wanting to do his part in the way he knew how, said, "Aunt Mollie, let me treat everybody tonight to a nice dinner back in town. I'm sure you've already done enough work for today."

But Mollie was quick to answer, "Oh no, Bruce, I won't hear to that. I've got things all prepared. Let's just have a nice supper right here." Then she grinned adding, "Bruce, we midwest farm people have 'supper.' It's the city folks that eat 'dinner' at night!"

To which Bruce replied, "Well, you're the boss, Aunt Mollie!" And, deep down he was relieved. He couldn't believe his feeling but he really didn't want to leave to go into town.

Mollie said, "I'll tell you what. Let's finish our coffee and our drinks and then the girls and I will go into the kitchen and start the ball rolling while you boys get your luggage carried in."

In explanation she added, "You kids will be using three of the several rooms that old Ethan had built in the front area of the upstairs. You'll recognize the ones when you see them. You're going to find that Tom and I have remodeled and refurbished only the rooms of this old house that we would be needing for our use. And, of course, we put in a pretty bathroom up there. So you can look those rooms over and you kids can decide whom takes which!"

Then she added, "Under the circumstances Tom and I couldn't see the point of keeping up this entire old place. That would have cost a fortune and our future here was uncertain. You see, years ago Ethan's needs were to accommodate large families and the many hired hands that were required in attending to the manual labors of his day. Since bedrooms were used for sleeping only, he built them small sized and furnished them sparsely. It was the kitchen and the dining room where he needed the space. So those were ample. The living room was never homey or comfortable and, of course, the parlor was used on very special occasions only. In those olden days parlors were strictly for show."

"But, I'll tell you what," Mollie added. "Tomorrow I'll give you a tour. I'll show you the novelties old Ethan built into this dream house of his! I think you'll all agree that he was quite a guy."

Mollie's suggestions sounded like a good plan. And the evening, which included an old-fashioned farm-type supper, got off to a pleasant start.

Sammie happily kept swishing that longhaired tail. Just like the long line of other collie dogs before him, beginning with Buddy, Billy Mitchell's dog of long ago, Sammie moved from place to place wanting to be near the laughter. All that laughter and light-heartedness was in part due to Mollie's being such a fun hostess. But, if those young people had asked her opinion, Mollie would have shared with them that deep down she always could sense the echoes of Ethan Bennett's exuberance and energy still bouncing around the environment. Mollie was sincere in believing that Ethan's Whispering Pines was still affected, with the house itself pleasantly exuding those echoes of the past.

TWENTY

Exploring Their Legacy

From the long habit of beginning her day early, Mollie was on the patio, there outside the kitchen, having another cup of morning coffee. And Sammie was sprawled beside her.

Slipping out of their bed quietly, leaving Gail to take advantage of her being able to sleep in, Bruce had showered, chosen a clean sport shirt and shorts, and come downstairs. Peeking out, he'd located Mollie. So pouring himself some coffee, he went out to join her.

The two agreed on the June morning's being perfect. Also agreeing that just coffee would be enough for now. Bruce said he could wait for breakfast until the others roused.

Sitting there, feeling so super after his comfortable night's sleep, Bruce said, "Aunt Mollie, I have to tell you, all this is so great! It's so peaceful out here in the country."

Looking out across the big barn lot to the south, he could see the field with its neat rows of green corn. The young stalks were not yet tall enough to cover the black soil between the rows. Even though he'd lived his life in the "Cornhusker State" of Nebraska, he had never before given much thought to a cornfield. Now he remarked, "Holy gees, you can just sit right here and watch that corn grow, can't you?"

Mollie smiled at that. "And, do you know what, Bruce? A little later on, on a still day, I actually will be able to hear it grow!"

Bruce looked at her quizzically.

"That's right. At this stage out there now, the new plants are putting their energy into getting their basic roots put down, getting a good start. But soon it will shoot up so fast that at times it will make loud, audible slippery-like, popping sounds. With the atmosphere just right, we can hear it! The left half of

220

that field had always been used as pastureland for the livestock. Then when Tom and I sold out and the fences and buildings were taken down, that piece of land was ready to produce extra good grain. So before long, I should be hearing lots of little growing spurts!"

"I thought you were kidding me, Aunt Mollie. I've never heard of that before!" Then, lazily, Bruce commented, "I swear, I believe I could just sit here like this all day."

"Oh, it is pleasant, all right. But, you know, Bruce, most people today just don't take the time for doing that. I think there's a simple secret for having a good life. No matter how busy he is a person should learn to stay attuned to the little things going on around him; like noticing a pretty flower, a little child, butterflies and hummingbirds, a special phrase, or a special happening. He should savor it and relish it. It becomes a memory lying dormant within him. Then, during those inevitable moments when things pile up and get hectic, it will be ready to recall and re-savor. Being able to do that gives a person balance and stability."

Mollie smiled at him, adding, "And I know this from experience. When a person gets old, having nice memories to draw from and to reminisce about keeps him from being lonely."

Bruce took a swallow of coffee, mulling that over. Then he said, "You know, I hadn't realized that I was so in need of a vacation! I guess Gail and I have been pretty tied up in just living and getting our kids grown up. We've kept pretty involved just tending to things from day to day. I guess I've never thought too much about our own 'tomorrow.' Of course, we do have our IRAs and our 401(K)s."

Mollie told him, "Well, I think that's pretty normal for kids of your generation, Bruce."

He said, "It must be pretty nice at your age, all retired and comfortable. And you seem to be in such good health. Now, for Gail and me, and all our friends, I tell you, Aunt Mollie, that big world out there has gotten crazy and it's so demanding. We're well aware of how shaky things are."

"Yes, how well I know. Especially last year, after that horrific day of September 11th! But, you know, Bruce, a long time ago, when Tom and I had our young family, we also had to face some shaky times. The whole country did. Now, maybe when measured and compared with the complicated and shocking conditions of today, they were way down on the scale. But to us, living our time, they were momentous.

"We had to sort things out, trying to consider what was best for us. I think it was always automatic that our little family came first, and with the good Lord's help, of course, we worked hard to keep our family strong. Then, we just handled everything as it came along."

Looking at Bruce, smiling, she said, "You know, our good Lord made this earth with so much natural wonderment, then enhancing it with giving us so many beautiful colors. With His doing that I think He means for us to enjoy it. I just know He wants us to be happy in it, and fill it with laughter." She stopped, adding sadly, "But when He gave us such freedom in making our own choices, it's too bad the choice of idiocy had to be sprinkled into the mix. That sure paved the way for problems and challenges. And, today, all that's gotten out of hand!"

Bruce chimed in with, "Well, the problems out there right now are sure big and scary. But, we have to trust in our leaders and hope they make the right choices."

"I know. And they need our prayers. But, Bruce, it's been encouraging to read about and see it on TV of how the bulk of our people are uniting against this outrage, especially all the stories about so many of our young people. Like Holly! Can you imagine my feelings when I read her essay in our newspaper? Her words should be an inspiration for her peers. She's right when she said *'never before in history has there been an era of such opportunities for the futures of teenagers.'*"

Here, Mollie paused. Then she added, "But there again, Bruce, as we said yesterday, it does all boil down to the fact that each teenager's choice pretty much hinges on just whom or what has influenced his early formative years. And that puts us right back into that all important 'square one'...a good family home!"

At that moment, Gail's voice interrupted them. "Well, good morning, you two! And just what are you guys up to on this beautiful morning?" she queried, setting her steaming mug of coffee on the patio table.

Sitting down, then, shifting herself a bit to get comfortable, she picked up her cup. Holding that mug between both hands, slowly, she sniffed the fragrance. All wrapped in the warmth of the sun, she drew in a deep breath of that morning atmosphere. Tasting a sip of that steaming coffee, Gail knew it was going to be a great day!

Bruce had watched that little display with his actually seeing Gail's facial expression relax and transform into a lovely aura of contentment. He was visibly touched. A feeling of pride and richness gushed through him. But, being that macho man, all he said was, "Well, so you finally decided to join the living!"

She grinned at her husband. "Well, believe me, I hated to get up. I laid back on my pillow, just thinking about it." She took another sip of her coffee, and looking at her aunt, she said, "Aunt Mollie, the luxury of getting to sleep in like this morning is something I don't get to indulge in very often. It was wonderful! That was truly a good night's sleep. With the breeze coming through the windows, bringing in the interesting noises of the night, it was so peaceful. Not a sound of traffic!"

Lovingly, Mollie smiled at Gail. "That's good to hear. And I do know what you mean about traffic sounds. Whenever my travels have involved cities, I definitely was aware of the contrast."

And Gail, sensing this fact for her aunt, remarked, "Oh, my gosh, you really would notice that, wouldn't you?" Then, remembering the evening before, she said, "By the way, Aunt Mollie, before I went to sleep last night, I heard some animal howl. Would you know what it might have been?"

"It was probably a coyote. We have them around. And foxes. And, of course, we always have 'possums and raccoons, but they're quiet as they slip around, foraging for food. Some nights the screech owls call, and now and then, I hear a hoot owl. They always sound as though they must be about ten feet tall!" Mollie laughed. She was used to all the noises of the night, but she always loved listening to them.

Then she said, "But it's nothing like it used to be. Life out here has changed so much, especially the nights. You know, growing up as I did so long ago, before electricity came into being for us, when night came it got dark. And I mean a black dark, over the entire countryside. But we were used to it and we knew to be prepared for it."

Mollie smiled, remembering about all that. "Getting the lanterns and the lamps filled with kerosene, or coal oil as we used to call it, was an important everyday task. And those smoky lamp chimneys and lantern globes had to be cleaned every day as well. If anyone needed to go outside for anything, he had to use a lantern. When darkness came, the work at the barn had to be done by lantern light. We just never knew anything else. That was our life back then."

Thinking about that, she added, "But, thank goodness, there's always been some wonderful genius like Thomas Edison who worked at making things better! How fantastic when cities began to 'light up!' Although, for us out here, that took awhile. But, gradually REA came into being. That was the Rural Electrification Association. But, there again, that took years of our waiting for it to reach this area. Once it did, though, all the farmers began to install poles for security lights. And the whole countryside lit up. It wasn't long then 'till the 'dusk-to-dawn' sensor came into being and we no longer had to turn those switches off and on! Now when you look out at night, it's hard to tell where town ends and country begins!"

About that time young Ethan emerged, coming out through the kitchen to join the group. Along with the usual "good mornings" and in answer as to how he slept, Ethan said, "I thought I heard a dog howl last night, but I don't think it was a dog."

Gail chimed in, "I heard it too, Ethan. Aunt Mollie says most likely it was a coyote. We don't hear things like that in the city, do we son?"

"Then, it was wild, right?" He was looking at Aunt Mollie. "If I'd been out there, would it'a hurt me?" he asked.

"Not really," Aunt Mollie smiled at him. "Unless you had it cornered, it would have run from you. There aren't that many of them around and at night they're just looking for food. Farmers with flocks of turkeys or chickens, or sheep, have to guard against them. Along with the foxes."

As usual, thoughtfully, Ethan remarked, "Cool." This would be one more thing to share with his friends back home. His experience with closeness to anything wild was limited to Omaha's Henry Doorly Zooland Jungle.

With that, Mollie began to get to her feet, gathering up the coffee pot and her empty cup, saying, "What do you say to our going inside now and seeing about some breakfast?"

Gail got to her feet, stretching and drawing in a big breath of air. Picking up her empty mug, she looked at Ethan, asking, "Was Holly up yet?"

"Uh-huh, she was in the shower when I came down," Ethan answered.

This was Bruce's cue to follow. He was ready for some breakfast.

TWENTY-ONE

Exhuming the Richness of Heritage

"Oh no, thank you, Aunt Mollie," Bruce waved away the platter with its two or three remaining little cinnamon rolls she was holding before him. "I am sitting here completely stuffed! And I'm not seeing myself getting any of it worked off today either." He smiled contentedly at her. "Aunt Mollie, you do really know how to cook an omelet."

She grinned at him, saying, "Well, I've had lots of years of practice."

Gail suggested, "Aunt Mollie, let me clear up these breakfast things. Holly can help me. And you tend to whatever you need to while we're doing it. Remember, you said last night that you would give us a tour of the place. I'm really looking forward to that."

Bruce agreed, offering to help. He said, "We'll spend another night with you and then in the morning we'll need to head back for home."

"All right. Just put the dirty dishes in the dishwasher. Then, while you kids are busy with that, I'm going to do like my mother used to do whenever she was to have a busy day. I'm going to put on a kettle of Great Northern beans."

The kids all looked at Aunt Mollie. "Let's just say that this will be a part of your tour of the past! I'd like to treat you to the kind of noon dinner just like the old cooks used to make. A kettle of beans tends to itself, so on any busy day that was the menu. Like on washday when washing clothes had to be done manually on the washboard. That was a tremendous all-day job, and that's how I grew up. So, today, we'll have beans. Only we'll call ours 'bean soup.' But, I'll put 'rivels' in it and that will keep it like the days of old."

"Rivels?" Gail said, and the kids looked at each other, quizzically.

"Yes, rivels," Aunt Mollie repeated. "My mother added those for special times. For the last twenty minutes or so of the cooking time, Mom would drop in pinches of a noodle-like mixture that she would have all mixed and ready. Each little pinch would be noodley, yellow, and so good, bubbling and floating around in the soup of those beans. Any meal with rivels was so special!"

Aunt Mollie went ahead, then, to explain. "Back then, each kitchen had its big wooden dough bowl with lots of flour in it. It was kept setting there, ready for kneading piecrust or bread dough, biscuits or noodles. So, on special bean days, Mom would beat up a couple of eggs, add a pinch of salt and a tad of water. Then she'd puddle that mixture in the middle of the flour in that big bowl. With her hands, then, she worked flour into the liquid until she ended up with a little mass of fairly dry dough of just the right consistency. Then, for those last twenty minutes or so, she'd pinch off tiny pieces from that ball of dough and drop them into the bean soup. And, we had rivels!"

And, in the excited way Aunt Mollie related this, she had those young people looking forward to that noon meal!

In short time the kitchen was in order. And a big-lidded kettle was setting on a burner of the electric range, over just enough heat to maintain a low boil. In it, the beans, amply covered with water, were sharing the pot with several slices of fresh boneless pork loin. Later, Mollie would remove the meat, dice it, and then add it back into the beans.

As Mollie was taking the little group on their tour, she was doing her best to make the place come alive. She wanted those kids mentally to capture how it must have been long ago when the former Ethan's dreams had become a reality.

To get those young people into a proper mood for appreciating Ethan's advanced intellect, she said, "Now kids, I want you to remember, all this took place long ago from 1866 to 1869. Ethan and his siblings had been born miles from here, over in Ohio. And that home was a one-room log house with a dirt floor. It had a make-shift loft with handmade small beds for sleeping, and they reached that loft by climbing up a ladder attached to one wall."

It wasn't hard for Mollie to interject reality into her descriptions. After all, with her own beginning during the last couple of years of the WWI days, she could relate personally to those old conditions.

Going on, "Ethan had raised his own family in a similar log house, only he'd put in a wooden floor. Of course, electricity for power hadn't yet been discovered. So work was done by hand, with the help of animals and using ingenuity. Ethan's head just had to be full of dreams!"

First she showed them the room off the kitchen that was intended as maid's quarters. Then she explained about the huge fresh water vat built below that floor that was kept filled through an underground pipe running in from the well in the barn lot. She said that during those earliest years, the vat had to be kept filled by Ethan or the farm hands using the manually operated pump there in the barn lot. And Ethan had rigged a control for the flow of water, either to send it through the pipe to the vat or for use there at the pump. And she explained about the small manually operated pump at the kitchen sink.

Mollie told those kids that for the general run of households of that time, such a modern system as Ethan's was unheard of. To his neighbors it was unbelievable.

Bruce was impressed with the "ice box room." Mollie couldn't inform him of when it was last used. She couldn't remember of her folks ever having harvested ice for it. But she did remember that due to the thick sawdust insulation, the room was always cool.

Holly and Gail smiled over Ethan's bathroom, trying to imagine anyone's being excited over it. The tub still set there, but Mollie explained that its drain hadn't worked for years. Although she did remember of having had baths in it herself when she was a little girl.

She told of an entry in Carrie's journal saying "Sometimes it's too much trouble to tote in all the water. But it's nice to have the privacy when taking an easier kind of bath, using a pan of water, a piece of soap, and a washrag. And I got just as clean!"

Mollie took them up the back stairway to the "hired hands" bedroom, then on up to the full sized attic. Here she explained how she and her siblings had spent many rainy days up there in play. She told of roller-skating around that big attic space with their dodging apple barrels.

Mollie said that modern shoe skates had not yet been invented. Back then the skates were made to attach to the wearer's own shoes. They had wheels with roller bearings and they were adjustable to fit within limited sizes. By removing a nut from a bolt midway of the skate, it could be manually adjusted for length. A special skate key could adjust the width at the ball of the foot, allowing the attached clamp on either side of the skate to tighten or expand to fit onto the overlap that was a part of the shoe soles of that time. There was a leather ankle strap for securing the back of the skate to the foot.

She told them too of the winter evening trips up there for getting a panful of apples from one of the barrels, setting there and smelling so good.

Back downstairs, in the dining room, Bruce was impressed with Ethan's ceiling rod with its twelve-foot swing for options of lighting. Ethan's metal basket was still suspended at the outer end, but Mollie assured them the kerosene lamp setting in it was for "décor" only.

In the back corner of the dining room, Mollie pointed out a door. It was of normal height, but only about eighteen inches in width. First, undoing a latch at the top, she swung the door open, exposing an elevator-like wooden box that was as tall and as wide as the door itself. Mollie said it was a "dumb waiter."

The open-fronted box with its several shelves still hung freely with its Ethan-rigged pulleys and heavy two inch ropes still intact. A cobweb or two made it obvious that Mollie wasn't using it.

She explained that years ago things needed to be taken to the cellar, like the many jars filled from canning, or left-over foods. They were set on the open shelves of the box. Then, by hand-manipulating the doubled strand of rope, the box would be lowered to the cellar floor level. Of course, someone had to go down the cellar stairs to unload the shelves.

Mollie said the cellar floor was the original dirt, so flat-topped rocks had been placed on the floor in that area. With the rocks remaining cool in that atmosphere, any containers of food setting on them would be kept cooled as well.

Next on the tour was the living room with the big bay windows across the front. Mollie pointed out that she and Tom had refurbished this room, laying new carpeting and making it comfortable. But she said they preferred to spend their evenings in the cozier dining room. Also the computer setup was in the dining room.

Then, as part of the back wall of the living room, were two solid wood double doors. Mollie swung them open, exposing the old-fashion parlor of the days of long ago. She hurried to explain, "It's not hard to see why these doors are kept closed. This room is one of the house 'has-beens'!"

She chuckled then, remembering, "But now, kids, I see these rooms differently than you are seeing it! When I was little, my grandparents and my folks hosted some pretty mean Saturday night dances in these two rooms! With these doors left open, the rugs rolled up and carried out, and the furniture set back along the walls, it made a good-sized dance floor. All the neighbors would be invited."

"There was always someone who could play a fiddle and someone who could 'call' for square dancing. The floor would be rough, of course, but Gram-ma always had cakes of paraffin that she used for sealing over the top of the homemade jelly after it was poured into the jars and cooled. So, they would shave off paraffin, dropping lots of it all over the floor. After some running and sliding back and forth across it by us kids, the floor would get real slick."

Mollie was smiling, remembering those old times. "Those were fun times, kids. Most of the people in those days were good dancers. And other than for church affairs, fun times had to be instigated. Remember, back then, even radios hadn't come into being for common household families until in 1920, let alone televisions!"

Hearing this, Holly and Ethan just looked at each other. Mollie could see disbelief reflecting from their faces, maybe even a hint of pity.

This prompted her to say, "Oh, now, wait a minute, you two. I'll bet it's even safe to say that we kids back then felt more excitement about things than the kids of today do. The very fact that we didn't have entertainment gadgets for family amusement was probably a plus for us. We had to create things to do. We did have cards, dominoes, checkers and chess. And we had lots of get-togethers."

Thoughtfully, then, she said, "Too often, today little kids aren't allowed creative playtime. No time for just dreaming! Kids' toy rooms are filled and feelings of appreciation and excitement could easily become emotions of the past."

Then, in a merrier tone, she said, "Now, back then, getting ready for one of those Saturday nights, with all the anticipation, each one's work seemed easier, even for us little kids as we did our chores.

"After an early supper, the guests would begin to arrive. When I was still pretty small, they would be riding in buggies or wagons. The men would tie the reins of the teams along the fence of the barn lot. And I seem to remember that my folks would have set out some bunches of hay along the fence so the horses could feed from them.

"Then, gradually, in the very early 1920s, a family would come driving an automobile. That would generally be a Model-T or Model-A Ford, but as I recall, those early cars took lots of maintenance.

"When we got our first Model-T, my dad always carried baling wire and a ball of binder twine for emergency repairs. He always had his toolbox and an extra fan belt or two. And on most trips we never got by without at least one flat tire. But there again, we were prepared with a jack, a manually operated tire pump, and a little kit with sticky patches to cover punctures in the inner tubes inside the tires.

"With our larger family and needing more room, Dad bought a two-seat open sedan Model-A Ford called a 'touring car.' It was equipped with a set of 'side curtains' to snap on during inclement weather."

Mollie was beaming, remembering those times. She continued then, "Gee, I'd better get back to those Saturday night dances or we'll be into our lunchtime! And, speaking of lunch, a food table would have been set up for those gatherings. My mom and my grandmother would have a special cake or something with hot coffee. And most of the neighboring women would bring cake or home-baked cookies or pies. There'd be something for everybody to drink."

Looking at Holly and Ethan, she added, "You know, kids, it was probably in these very rooms that your great-grandfather learned how to dance. 'Way back when he was just a little boy."

The next segment of the tour took them outdoors. Bruce and Gail had not yet seen the outside from this angle, and the very size of that big yard impressed them. Their own city lawn was dwarfed in comparison.

The entire yard was still fenced in with regular farm-type woven wire attached to wooden posts. The yard was bounded along the west by the road, and the big square three-story house set in the middle of it, with its front facing that road. The yard was still well shaded by tall stately trees, but only a few of them were the original maples set out by Ethan Bennett.

Even the road along the front was changed from Ethan's time. It wasn't just dirt like in the olden days, and it was no longer solidly lined on both sides with maple trees. Now it was a well-maintained blacktopped mile with only a tree here and there along the fence lines.

Mollie and her guests had stepped out from the dining room onto the porch and now she led them down the two porch-wide steps and out into the yard. From there, they turned to look back at the front of the house.

This had been Mollie's home forever and she wanted to impart her pride and sentiment to these kids. These kids were heirs to this segment of their history. Only through her eyes could they glimpse into this portion of their past. And she so wanted them to get the feel of the vibrancy that was coursing through her own being.

Just a couple of summers before, Mollie had hired the house painted, using the same warm gray with white trim that she'd always remembered. Gesturing now with a swing of her hand, "Considering that Ethan had never known anything but a small log house back in Ohio, isn't this something?"

Jutting out at the mid-front was the three-sectioned bay window of the living room, flanked on either side by the identical porch. Each open porch was roofed over to join up with the bay window. And each had the full porch-width two steps.

"And now, I want you to notice the landscaping," Mollie said, "I've read all those old journals giving the history of how all this place came about. I'm sure you guys are going to want to read about it also. Nothing is said about any particular plan for landscaping, and maybe Ethan just followed whims as he saw opportunities. But I think you'll agree that these brick-edged path patterns of his are pretty unique. Knowing Ethan, he didn't settle for the customary plain old path going down through his yard."

There before them, they could see the beginning of Ethan's landscaping design. And turning then, to look toward the road, those young people could see what Mollie meant. Ethan's landscaping of the front yard was indeed quite impressive.

Starting at the lower step of each porch began a brick-edged wide path that narrowed to about 36 inches, then joined mid-way of the bay window section, thus making a semi-circle that extended out about ten feet from the house. From that junction point, it became a single path leading toward the road. It ran for about thirty feet where it became a 3-way junction.

Here a walker would have some options. He could follow the path straight ahead or he could follow a semi-circle path to the right, or a semi-circle path to the left. Then about fifty feet or so ahead was where the semi-circles completed to form another 3-way junction. From that point the path on to the road gate was again single.

Mollie went on, "Just think, these are the very same bricks that Ethan put here. Notice how he laid them. Probably he dug a little trench first, outlining the paths. Then, one brick at a time, he angled each brick in, long side up, allowing the one end to jut up. Just look at the way he laid those bricks that way, in one continuous line, with the top one-third of one brick resting on the lower one-third of the next one. Can you imagine how many bricks all this has taken? I'm sure that Ethan bought the bricks, but in those days each brick was made by hand."

Mollie paused then, saying sort of sadly, "Oh, but how I wish you kids could have seen this as I remember it. You see, once the paths with the brick edgings were done, Ethan outlined each of these semi-circles by setting out some kind of flat-foliaged, low-growing evergreen shrubs. I think they might have been some kind of cedar. I remember that those shrubs were still there as I was growing up. But at some point, they got old and raggedy, beginning to die out and no one ever replaced them."

She smiled, and then adding, "Now, there is one thing that I do know for sure. I've run for miles and miles around these paths in this yard!"

Then looking at Holly and young Ethan, she added, "And your great-grandfather, too. He did his share of playing and running on these paths too!"

As Mollie talked, those four were taking in the design of the paths with their beginning at the two porches and ending at the white picket gate in the fence at the road. It was a good 150 feet, probably more, down to that gate.

Suddenly Gail spoke up, saying, "Hey, wait a minute! I'm part of that history too. I did some running around here when we visited that time when I was little! Don't you remember, Aunt Mollie?"

They all laughed at that. "Of course, you did, Gail. You're right; you are a part of the history! Maybe the kids will do a little running before the day is over so they can remember it as well."

"Way to go, Mom," and Ethan gave his mother an okay smile.

Continuing then, Mollie's voice held excitement as she said, "Anyway, kids, just imagine! A hundred and thirty-some years ago, with all of the other stuff that man had to take care of in getting this place set up, he still took time to make things special!"

Then adding further, "And he didn't have any machines to help him. Everything was pretty much done by hand. But, when you read the journals, you'll see that he hired lots of men to help with the labor. Gosh, how I've always wished that I could have known him!"

Next, Mollie walked the group cat-a-cornered down the yard to the left where a broken circle of tall, large-girthed pine trees stood. Bruce wondered about their position and why they were in such a haphazard design. The trees seemed almost to form a circle, but there were such uneven gaps between them.

Mollie had an explanation, "Now kids, this is what remains of Ethan's outdoor 'screen room.'" Those kids just looked at her, waiting.

"This too is all explained in Carrie's old records. In the beginning Ethan set out enough trees to make a full circle. And when they grew tall enough, he built a screened-in structure with a frame of wood to fit inside the circle. It had a screen door. Carrie tells about how the family would sit in it during the summer and into fall, until it got too chilly. Sometimes they'd enjoy a special meal, all bug-free. And she tells about its being a safe, cool place in which to leave a baby in its cradle."

Then Mollie got all wistful. "But this is the best part. Carrie wrote about how her dad explained this part of his dream for this place. He said he always loved to hear the wind whooshing through the tops of pine trees. He said to him it always sounded like the trees were whispering. So he made this a special pine tree circle and he named this homestead 'Whispering Pines'!"

Grinning, then, Mollie confided, "Now, kids, I know I get a little dramatic, maybe I even get a bit silly, but I love coming out here. When I'm quiet, and if there's a breeze blowing, I too can hear the whooshing. I even imagine that I can hear happy laughter." Mollie paused, then she let out a little chuckle, as if she felt the need to break the intenseness of the moment.

"Anyhow," she added then, "I just know there's always a good feeling about this little area!"

Those kids were visibly touched. Gail, especially, was affected by her aunt's words. The thought had suddenly hit her, *maybe that's the feeling I've been sensing when I'm in our dining room area at home. It's those candlesticks!*

She was quick to say, "Oh, Aunt Mollie, that is so beautiful! Before we leave, I'm going to come out here, and I'll be real quiet. Maybe I'll be able to hear it too!"

Eleven-year old Ethan sidled up to his mother, saying, "I want to come with you, Mom."

Gail put her arm around her son, hugging him to her.

Looking at her wristwatch, then, Mollie noted it was about 10:30. "I think we have time to take a quick check of the back yard. And then I'll have to go in and get my barn door remote so we can go out to see the barn. I'll bet you kids need a break, maybe a drink of something."

She'd been steering them across the front yard and toward the back of the house as she spoke.

Once back there, they could see the big orchard abutting the back fence. And they could see that most of the trees there were showing the neglect as she'd already explained. Like the rest of Ethan's Whispering Pines, it too was succumbing to the demands of a changing era.

As they crossed the path leading to the outhouse and the orchard gate, Mollie was heading them along toward the east side of the house. Reaching the back veranda area, she called their attention to the big black bell suspended from a sidearm attached to a ten-foot pole.

"Now, this bell was another source of pride of Ethan's. As you can recognize, it's kinda like a small replica of the big Liberty Bell in Independence Hall in Philadelphia. I do recall that during my parents' time here, the pole had to be replaced along with the supporting arm."

"Well, I'm not surprised," Bruce commented, walking around the pole, admiring the set-up. "That dude's got some weight to support."

"Not only was the bell decorative, but it was helpful as a means of communication. I grew up hearing that resounding bong as it was rung to signify some happening. A bong would mean it was time for the hired men to get washed up for noontime dinner. Or if my dad heard it sounding a time or two during oft meal times, he knew he was needed at the house."

With this probing around in her mind, Mollie was remembering another incident. And she thought these kids would be interested. "Let me tell you about the important role this old bell played in one summer afternoon scene in the 1920s. I was a kid about your age, Ethan, but I don't think I'll ever forget my feeling of the stark terror connected with that day."

"A neighbor from a mile or so north of us came down the road galloping on his horse, and as he neared our place he was yelling, 'Craig's house is on fire!' Repeating it over and over! I can still feel the cold chills. Things got busy real fast, I can tell you. Team operation took over. My dad and bigger brothers along with a couple of hired hands ran to our Model-A Ford touring car. They didn't even notice me piled in with them! Dad jumped behind the steering wheel, and as the Ford chugged out the gate, my mom was already at this bell. She was steadily pulling the rope. With the reverberation of this deep bong, bonging rippling across the countryside, the SOS was resounding. That, of course, set the party lines of those old wooden telephones to humming inside all the neighbors' farm houses and the neighborhood was alerted. Whew! I swear, I can still hear it, even after all these years. But, you kids probably already know the answer. With only the 'bucket brigade' dousing of the water from the horse tank available for fighting it, it was just in no way any match against those wicked flames.

"With sinking hopelessness, the Craig family along with that little gathering of neighbors had to stand back, just watching, as that old wooden 2-story home was consumed. The family and the earliest of those arriving neighbors had managed to get out a few things, but for the most part everything was lost. And, of course, in those days, having insurance of any kind was an unknown option for common folks."

Mollie could see that her audience was somewhat moved. She was unaware that in that setting, with all that isolation and quiet stretching out all around them, it had been easy for those four Omaha city people to step back with her in time; make them sense having a part in her portrayal.

Checking her watch, then shaking her head in self-admonition, "My goodness, how I do seem to digress!"

With that, Bruce too, shook his head slowly from side to side, blinking, looking at the ground. "Holy gees, how we people today do take things for granted..."

And the tour continued.

While they were still there at the back door area, Mollie explained about the huge rainwater vat below the surface of the veranda. "Ethan's family used an old style hand pump to get water from it. But, after electricity was run to this area, our men rigged the means to get the water from the tap there where the hose is attached. I only use the water now for my flowers."

She smiled, and then admitting, "I've become one of today's women like everyone else. I get my hair done in town, my meats and vegetables from the grocery, and I haven't carried a bucket of water for some time now!"

As they walked, she pointed to where at one time there had been the berry patch, the little smoke house, and the garden area. Then closer toward the barn lot, the old cob and coalhouse and a poultry house were still standing.

The fencing for the poultry pen was gone and now, of course, those remaining buildings were neglected and empty.

Mollie said, "It's only been since Tom's death that I haven't used that chicken house. It was pretty convenient to have our own eggs and chickens to eat. With the price of feed, though, I'm sure it was never cost-effective."

"Oh but Aunt Molly, those chickens would be alive! That meant that every time you wanted to cook a chicken you had to kill it and dress it, didn't it?" Gail was serious.

"Well, yes," Mollie smiled at her. "But remember, I grew up with that. We thought nothing of it. And our chickens were better tasting than the ones of today. They were more muscular and healthy, scratching and picking on the ground for food. And they certainly were always fresh!"

Gail grimaced, "My gosh, I wouldn't know what to do with a live chicken. And besides, I'd never have the time."

"Well kids, remember I learned to prepare foods and cook long before packaged poultry in stores came into being. At first, of course, they were unwrapped, whole, and kept cool by being packed in ice. And you should have heard our complaints as those first packaged ones became available. We didn't like the way the pieces were cut up. Some weren't recognizable as our usual chicken parts," Mollie was laughing, remembering those times.

Again, as they'd been talking, she'd been steering them back to the side of the house. Stopping then, she said, "Okay, Bruce, see that trap door panel up there in the side of the house? That's above the icebox room. Ethan's men could use that doorway to store the blocks of ice they cut from the frozen pond."

Here Mollie had to smile, shaking her head. She said, "I think that ice room sort of blew the people's minds around here! I guess Ethan had quite a reputation!"

Then she said, "Okay, I'm going in the house now and get my remote. And I'll check the bean kettle. You guys take a little break and then we'll go see the barn."

The girls went inside with Mollie. Grinning at each other, the boys decided they'd make another visit to the old outhouse.

With Ethan and Holly going over the stile and Sammie right behind them, the others chose to walk through the gate. Then going out into the barn lot, they paused by the big empty horse tank. To those city kids, that big rectangular vat could pass as an above ground swimming pool.

But Mollie was explaining, "This tank used to be a busy area. It was the watering hole for the animals. But now, with no animals around, there's no need for keeping water in it. Today it would be only a breeding place for mosquitoes."

Then she explained about the 5' x 5' wooden platform by the tank. She said, "There's a well pit beneath this. Ethan's original well is down there. Throughout the long span of time, the pipes have had to be pulled and replaced a time or two. And, of course, now there's an automatic pump down there in the pit. But, Bruce, I'll bet you know more about things like that than I do. I'm not too mechanically-minded."

But Bruce just gave a little laugh, saying, "Aunt Mollie, remember I'm a city boy. I get my water by turning on a faucet!"

"Right," and she smiled at him, adding, "And, how thankful I am that those old days of hand pumping are long gone. That was hard work and so time consuming."

Remembering, she just shook her head. Then, "Kids, I want you to click onto your imagination channel. Let's pretend for a moment. Let's flash back a hundred and thirty some years ago! Just think! We're standing here in Ethan Bennett's barnyard. This is the same fenced-in area that he laid out in the beginning. When all his fantastic plans were still dreams dancing around in his head."

She had those kids' attention, and her excitement was contagious. "Now I want you to keep in mind that, at first, all this was just open country that Ethan had chosen under the Homestead Act. Over in Danville, in the county seat land office, all this was on map pages, marked off in 160-acre, quarter sections. But out here, everything was wide open and covered with tall prairie grass. Ethan had a lot of clearing off to do.

"Can't you just hear the crackling of the open fire as he and his RoseMarie sat around it, laying out those beginning plans?

"Their new-found friend, Billy Mitchell, with his collie dog, Buddy, was here with them. Then Ethan's mom and dad came from Ohio to help. And men were hired on for the huge undertaking. Ethan decided to build this barn first." Mollie gestured toward the barn.

"Everyone, the family and the hired men, camped out right here in the open. They cooked, ate, and slept right out here until the barn was finished. Then the family members lived in it until the house was done.

"Ethan hired enough men to work on each individual project of his whole plan, so everything pretty much got finished all at the same time. And as a building got finished, Ethan brought in the particular livestock to go in it."

Pointing over to the northeast corner, she said, "As plans shaped up, over in that corner was a granary. It had partitions to make three bins, with a door to each partition. The bins were for storing the harvested grains like oats and wheat. Then there was a farm gate in that back fence line, opening into the big pasture. And toward the other corner was a huge cow barn. Up the other side, on the south, toward that cornfield, was the pig barn with a pen. And, of course, the way the main barn there was built with its different levels, the horses had the lower part for their shelter.

"Then, placed out this way from the cow barn, there was a big corn crib. That crib was a typical kind with an open driveway through the middle separating two crib areas for storing ear corn. Open spaces were left between each one of the boards on the sides of the cribs so the ears of corn could get air circulation. When the frosts came in the fall, and the corn in the fields was matured, those hardened ears were hand-shucked and tossed into the wagons. Then it was hauled here and stored in these cribs."

Mollie paused. "Sorry kids, I do tend to get carried away when I talk about those old times! But, you know, I actually did live all of this myself. The buildings I just described were all here. And they were filled with animals.

"Standing here, talking about it, I'm remembering those evenings when I was a young kid and how pleasant they were. Suppertime would be nearing. Everyone was getting hungry, wanting to get the chores done, to get the day's work behind them. The air was reverberating with the sound of animals. The cows were bawling, wanting to be milked. There were squeals from the pigs. And young colts would be scampering and whinnying, and there would be some bleating amongst the sheep in the pasture. Each of those animals too was looking forward to being fed and being readied for the night."

Drawing in a big breath, smiling, "Gosh, I can still sense the smells blending in with all those sounds. And, hovering over all this was such peacefulness, such a wonderful contentment. I swear I can still feel it."

Mollie hesitated, quietly, looking at those young people. Then she added, "I'm aware now of how privileged I and my siblings were, being subjected to all that olden, everyday simplicity. I realize now that interwoven within that serenity and peacefulness was a trait called 'dignity'."

Once more she hesitated, glancing at Ethan. His young face was reflecting serious interest in the mental picture she'd just created. Giving him a special smile, she said, "Ya know, Ethan, at your age, if I'd been told that, probably I'd have been scared to death, thinking I was coming down with a bad disease or something."

Mollie smiled, hearing the little ripple of laughter, then, "Anyway, I can see now that, unknowingly, we kids were being programmed in with a stability that strengthened us. And we would draw on that quality to get us through any adult rough times ahead."

"Oh, Aunt Mollie," Gail expressed, "how wonderful to hear you tell these things. Thank you. You're making all this come alive for us. Why, even I could see and hear the animals as you talked. I felt like I was part of it!"

"That's good, Gail." Mollie was sincere. "But a glimpse into the past like this can make you realize just how fantastic life today is. Believe me, I've never wanted to go back to those old times. I'll take the conveniences of today anytime."

Looking at her watch, then, "Let's get this barn checked out," and she began steering her guests toward the incline leading up to the barn's second level. Responding to Mollie's pressing the overhead door opener in her hand, the wide door began to rumble as it slowly rolled upward in its tracks.

As the little group walked up the incline, with Mollie's car coming into view, Bruce gave a little laugh, remarking, "Well, Holy gees, Aunt Mollie, I can't believe this! I fully expected to see a zippy little red car!"

"Now Bruce. Those are for the young gals. I stuck to the conservative new 'gold.' But, I will admit to having a heavy foot. I've always loved to drive." Adding, "Old Ethan would never have suspected that such a contraption as an automobile would ever occupy his barn, would he?

"It was pretty ingenious on his part to build into this hill the way he did. The family lived on this floor until the house was finished, then it became a work place as well as storage area for things like the harness and the tools.

"The horses had stalls on the ground level below, while the hay was easily accessible from the mow above, and the straw from the straw barn there beyond that wall. Ethan had his workable plan all figured out. And he built this barn well for it to be still standing in such good condition after all these years."

Mollie turned to young Ethan and Holly. "Kids, see that ladder built over there on the wall? Can you see that it comes up the wall from below, through the opening there in the floor and goes on up through that opening into the hay mow? That was so whoever was tending chores, feeding or bedding down the horses, he could climb that ladder, and with a pitchfork, toss down the hay through those openings. Clear down to the barn level below us. Now, do you see that other big opening up there in the sidewall of the haymow? It opens out over the straw barn. Okay, now, can you picture your great-grandfather and me as young kids like you? We'd climb up that ladder up into the haymow. Then, standing in that big opening up there, we'd make a flying leap, diving down onto the big pile of straw there in the straw barn! Now, that was some kind of fun, believe me!"

Ethan looked at Holly. His eyebrows wrinkling up in a wide-eyed look, he said, "Wow!"

"Remembering that straw pile," Mollie explained, "during harvest season when the oats and wheat were being threshed and the new straw was blown in, the pile would be so high that it made a short jump. But as fall and winter feedings and beddings took the pile down, those jumps became more exciting. I'd never thought about it before, but that straw pile wasn't very high by the time of the next harvest. I guess we kids were somehow smart enough to know better than to jump then. We could have broken out necks! Well, anyway, none of us ever got hurt!"

Laughingly, Bruce and Gail just shook their heads.

Enjoying the reaction, Mollie said, "Well, today, this makes a good garage, although at times, it seems pretty far from the house."

Gail said, "I was thinking that, Aunt Mollie, Especially when it's raining."

"I keep a lot of umbrellas, Gail. Two or three in the car and as many in the house."

Then Gail asked, "Do you drive at night? Aren't you afraid, coming in late and making the long trip to the house?"

"Well, yes, I still drive at night. I have friends in town and I belong to different organizations. But as long as I have Sammie, I'm not afraid. I call him my 'barometer!' As long as he meets me, wagging his tail, I am confident. That assures me there is no one around. And sometimes, if it's real late, I do leave the car setting by the stile until morning."

Mollie checked her wristwatch again. She said, "Okay, guys, the tour's over. It's dinnertime! And it's going to take about 35 minutes 'til 'table time'."

Twenty-two

Relaxing and Re-capping

By mid-afternoon once again the little group had gathered together on the patio outside the kitchen area. The noontime meal with the old-time rivels had been a pleasant success and now the kitchen was back in neat order.

They were content in just lazily sprawling there in the warm June sunshine. Mollie had brewed a fresh pot of coffee for the three grown-ups and Holly and Ethan had cold cans of cola.

Now that Gail and her family had gotten acquainted with the place itself and learned so much of their ancestors' beginnings, those young people were full of further questions for Mollie.

Gail smiled at her aunt, remarking with sincerity, "What a privilege you've given us, going to all this trouble in arranging our coming out here like this. My gosh, just think what we would've missed in all this personal family genealogy had you never contacted us like you did. I'll love you forever for it, Aunt Mollie!"

"And I agree with her," Bruce was quick to say. "Only, Gail, you're just not putting enough emphasis on that word 'privilege.' Now the subject of history has never been my forte, but, Aunt Mollie, I want to tell you that in listening to you these couple of days, you've given my little world a good shaking up. It's going to take a few days for me to get everything sorted out. Now there's one thing I do know for sure. The next time I hear the fire trucks sounding their sirens, I'm not going to lose any time in helping to clear the street for them…. and the ambulances as well. Today it seems that too many have become calloused and show irritated annoyance when anything, even a red stop light, interferes with their selfish and narrow personal doings."

Then, with a little shake of his head, "Talk about a history channel! We've sure been accessed into a live one. Or maybe it was a live 'show and tell.' I've read a lot of articles about aging and changes and so forth, but to me it was merely statistical and I never really retained a lot of it." He paused, in appreciative thought, taking a drink of coffee.

Then he went on, "Aunt Mollie, I've watched Holly and Ethan as they've listened to your talk about your life and the olden times. Along with all that, once we've read those old parchment journals, the kids'll have their own personal library of material for themes and essays. You've introduced them to ideas and substances more interesting than a lot of the empty drivel offered on too much of today's TV."

"Well, kids," Mollie said, "Your responding like you have in all of this has meant a lot to me, that's for sure. I've always been a firm believer that older people are obligated to see that family heritage is handed down through the generations. My own mother always boasted of having been blessed with some of those two Carrie Bennetts' genes."

Bruce spoke up, "Well, look who else got a good share of those genes as well! I like hearing your stories and the way you describe those olden times and ways. You've certainly made them come alive for us. And now, of course, we can say that Holly also shares in that special gene department!"

Mollie looked appreciatively at him, saying, "Thank you for all that, Bruce. I'm sure that sometimes I'm guilty of too much storytelling. But olden times are fun to reminisce about. A sad thing is when young people wait too long in asking about the personal things of their background. They wait until their relatives are too old and incapacious or even gone. It's fairly easy to track down one's family genealogy, but that's just cold facts. One can learn of the personal things only from the older relatives who lived them."

For a moment, Mollie paused thoughtfully, then added, "I'm always glad that you young people have all these fantastic conveniences of today. I'm sure glad I'm getting to enjoy so many of them. Of course, new problems come with them, but just like in those olden times, there are those with inventive fertile minds who come up with the answers."

Gail, in a somewhat wistful tone, said, "Aunt Mollie, what you said a minute ago about waiting too long makes me know how much I've missed in not being closer with my grandparents. But it's good to know about my own grandfather's being a part of all the stories you've told us of your childhood. I can't remember of his ever talking too much about this place or his boyhood during any of the times that I was with him. Although I do vaguely remember our visit here that time when I was a little girl."

With an affectionate smile for her niece, Mollie said, "Well, Gail, for me this old place echoes in memories of your grandfather and my other siblings. What a wonderful life we had here," and her face was reflecting a soft endearing sentiment as she was shaking her head from side to side, thinking about those things of years ago.

She went on, "And all that hard work built strength and character, I guess. Remember this morning out there in the barn lot when I was talking about the old corncrib that used to stand out there? Well, Gail, your grandfather could have told you incidents about that better than I could. For several winters before he left the farm here he had to help with getting the corn out of the fields and into that crib. And back then, let me tell you, corn husking meant hard work!"

Again she had those kids' attention. "It would begin about the time of the first frost and our dad always hoped to have it finished by New Year's Day. It was done in cold weather because the corn shucked easier and, too, that was when the corn was ready for harvesting. The frosts would come by mid or late September and we'd always begin to get snows early in November.

"Our winters remained colder then and we had more snow in those days. So, with it not getting warm enough to melt it, the snows stayed on the ground and kept piling up, one on top of another, and it would get pretty deep. Between the snows, a crust would freeze over the top. All of us had sleds and ice skates and lots of families owned sleighs. A horse or a team could pull a sleigh right over the top of the snow. Today, of course, snowmobiles have taken over."

They all nodded in agreement on that.

Mollie went on, then, "A lot of preparation had to be done before the corn harvesting started. I'm sure you kids have noticed the wagons used on the farms of today. Of course they've been modernized with smaller wheels and rubber tires and a better way to empty them. The old ones had tailgates, but there was lots of hand scooping involved! Our old wagons were about the same size as now and the grain beds were about the same depth. Back then the men would slip a sideboard down over the top rim of one side of the wagon, extending that side upward maybe 40 inches or so. These were called 'bang-boards.'

"Once the corn was ready, a man planned to be in the field soon after daylight, ready to go. He would be warmly dressed. He'd have on husking gloves, or maybe mittens, and then he would strap a 'husking hook' on his wrist. Walking the cornrow on the opposite side of the bang-board, he would jerk an ear off the cornstalk, quickly slitting down that corn husk with that hook, then with practiced dexterity, rip off that husk and pitch the bare ear toward the bang-board. As it hit the bang-board, dropping into the wagon, he already had the next ear jerked off. And his team of horses stood patiently, waiting for his order to inch ahead.

"Whew," Mollie laughed. "It tires me just to talk about it! I can still hear those nubbins hitting those bang-boards. With the atmosphere so clear and cold, and with all the neighboring farmers in their fields, the air reverberated with those thuds as those hard corn ears hit those boards. And each man had a goal of getting his second load by noontime.

"Each load had to be taken to the barn lot to be stored in the crib. And, of course, by my time, gasoline engines were used to power an elevator contraption to get the ears up into the cribs.

"Built into the mid ridge row of the part of the roof over each crib was a cupola. That was a roofed-over, dog house-like structure, built over an opening in the main roof of the crib. With the portable 18-inch or so wide elevator beginning at ground level, it slanted upward to the opening in the cupola. The powered elevator track worked sort of like today's escalators. It was an endless tin belt with a 2-inch or so high ridge placed every couple of feet or so to hold the ears in place as they moved upward, dropping them off through the hole in the roof. And there was always some scooping involved at the ground level, as well as some leveling-off of the dropping ears inside the crib.

"I should mention that some of the wagon loads were taken into one of the nearby towns to a huge grain elevator to sell for needed ready cash. Or, if a farmer was having a bad year, he might have pre-sold his entire crop and would haul all of it into the elevator. Sort of like having a mortgage on his crop, I suppose, and he would have to deliver to settle up," Mollie explained.

Pausing, taking a swig of coffee, thoughtfully, she added, "With today's machinery, all that has changed. With the developing of hybrid corn, it matured earlier, and corn pickers were invented for harvesting. Now, with the huge machines with their air-conditioned and heated cabs, corn is picked, husked, and shelled in one operation as the machine moves through the field. And those machines take a wide swathe of rows at a time."

Mollie laughed then, adding, "Of course, they take quite a swathe out of a bank account, too!"

Again, Mollie just shook her head, saying, "All this is good. Being a farmer today is a regular career, with vacations and health benefits, like city folks! The work in those olden days was so hard, and so slow. But, I'm sure that the folks of those times were just as happy as ones living today. I guess each generation just lives!"

Thoughtfully, Bruce looked at her. He said, "Aunt Mollie, you really have seen a lot of changes, haven't you? It's amazing."

"Well, Bruce, that's true. You know, though, some of today's older people tend to dwell on only the pleasant parts of those old times. They don't clutter their memories with all that backbreaking hard work that was involved. Some even say they'd like to go back! I think they are remembering those cheap prices on everything while forgetting they had very little money with which to buy them!"

Young Ethan spoke up, asking, "How did that first Ethan get his corn crop harvested?"

For a moment Mollie mulled that over a bit, then she said, "You know, I can't really answer that. The fact that he built the crib tells us he stored it. And he did build the row of bins in the kitchen for holding 100-pound bags of flour and the other staples. Work animals were used to power the mills to grind the wheat and the corn for meal."

Mollie halted a moment then she said, "Do you know what, Ethan, I remember reading in one of Ethan's daughter's writings about that. You'll be able to read it yourself. She tells about a team of horses being hitched to the gear apparatus that empowered the elevator that carried the ear corn up to the cupola of the crib. The team was kept walking around and around in a circle, forcing that big rotating gear to turn."

She smiled, reminded of another thing. "Even in my time, I remember our father saved out enough of his best ears of corn for seed. It was then our whole family got involved in shelling the grains off those seed corncobs by hand. Now, for us kids, that was a business! Dad paid us a penny an ear for that shelling. So each of us kept track of our own account."

Mollie laughed, remembering. She added, "Oh, yes, and each winter we had to shell off our pop corn from the cobs, too. After the men had brought the ears in from the field, they would shuck back the husks on each ear without detaching them. Then, holding several ears by the husks, they'd tie them in clusters and hang them up in the attic to dry."

"A penny an ear! What could you do with a penny?" Holly was amazed. "My friends toss them away!"

"Yes, I know," Mollie said, "And we older people pick them up. In our day a penny would buy a lot of things. And, too, we recite that little verse, '*See a penny, pick it up, all the day, you'll have good luck.*' I don't know about the luck, but at least it brings a smile!"

Holly smiled too, saying, "I'll have to remember that."

Then Ethan said, "Aunt Mollie, you've talked a lot about work. What did you do for fun when you were a kid, besides jumping in the hay mow?"

"Well, we didn't have any action toys, so we played action games that involved us physically! We had to use our imagination to create ways to play. One thing we loved to do was to run a hoop. My siblings and I have run for miles around the paths of this place doing that. And I've still got good leg muscles from that beginning all those years ago!

"Maybe you kids have never seen a hoop! That was the little iron ring, about 10 inches or so in diameter, that was used on the hub of a wagon wheel to strengthen it. And wagon wheels were always breaking down, so we had a good source of hoops. Then, with the narrow slats of wood called laths that were used in building, like in walls for anchoring plaster, or in latticework, we had a good outlet for getting them.

"We would measure and saw a piece of lath according to our individual height, and then nail a 12-inch piece across the bottom end of it, forming an upside down 'T.' Then, grasping that framework in our right hand, with our left hand we'd carefully let our hoop roll down the narrow slat to the ground with our taking off after it. We'd run along, adeptly nudging and guiding our hoop, keeping it rolling, and maneuvering its direction by that short cross piece of lath. Now, believe me, there was an art to accomplishing this. But, practice made us good at it. I remember taking great pride in controlling that little hoop."

"Oh, yes, and we kids kept a good string of 'riding horses!' Now, those were something else."

Mollie had to chuckle about that. "You see, with all the men's regular work, there wasn't time to waste on summer mowing of the roadsides as farmers do today. Consequently, certain weeds along the ditches grew to heights of 6 or 8 feet tall, and the straight stems of them would be tough and hard, and have a cluster of bushy leaves at the tops. Now, with our imaginations, they made excellent horses. We'd cut a tall weed, then trim off the foliage, leaving only the bushy end. That would become the horse's tail. Then, using a length off Dad's big ball of binder twine, we fashioned a bridle and a loop for reins on the 'head-end.' We'd christen it with a name, and, voila, once astraddle of that, holding those reins, we had a riding horse!"

Then, Mollie gestured toward the woven wire fence separating the barn lot from the yard. She said, "See all the open squares in the fence? Well, each of us would stake off our own 'barn area' along the fence, and each square would be a stall for a horse. When not riding, we'd rest the horse's head-end in the little stall.

"And each of us had our own string, with a name for each horse. I remember, sometimes we'd work to peel off patches of the outer weed covering to make a pinto colored horse.

"Talk about imaginations! Sometimes we'd be competitive, staging a race. Astraddle one of those fine steeds, quite often I could cross a finish line ahead of a sibling!"

Sipping some more swallows of coffee, smiling, remembering, she went on, "Sometimes we would make up and play out little situations...today those would be called 'skits,' I guess."

Mollie explained, then, "Those things would be some of our play on the fair-weathered summer days. On rainy days or in bitter cold wintertime, we'd have to play inside the house.

"I remember our sometimes going on an African 'safari.' Now, I believe every household back in that time owned a long, chaise lounge-type couch with a raised, rolled, full-width headrest. In elite society these were termed 'fainting couches,' but to us, out here in the country, ours was just a couch. It was upholstered in quilted, horsehide leather. And always black. For us kids, it became a perfect vehicle for containing our wild animals.

"Our imaginations turned two dining room chairs into a team of horses, and sitting excitedly on that raised couch end seat, we drove that team to Africa. In the face of great danger, we filled that back part of the couch with wild, African 'eaters,' and then we had to make that perilous trip back home! Such a trip would take a couple of hours!"

Mollie's audience was laughing along with her. She looked at Ethan, saying, "Gosh, we sure could have used you. I'll just bet that you'd have been real good at wrestling a tiger."

"Let me tell you, kids," Mollie added. "Those were fun times for us. We were shielded from the strife in the big world around us, like the period following WWI, and the leading up to the crashing of the stock market. Here on the farm we had our own food. And we were each so healthy. We were almost never sick."

Then, smiling, remembering, she said, "With the women in each household required to do so much sewing, there was always an abundance of empty thread spools. Those spools were made of lightweight wood and were more durable than the ones of today. Gail, I recall a feat of engineering constructed of empty thread spools on the side of the cob house building. And the engineer of that was your grandfather."

Mollie explained, "My brother must have been about ten when he'd used various lengths of binder twine to make several circular 'belts.' Or some of his belts were an inch wide cut across a discarded rubber inner tube, making a circle like a rubber band of today. Empty thread spools were his 'pulleys.'

"To begin his operation, he'd placed one end of the first belt on an actual metal pulley fastened to a hand-turned crank apparatus that he salvaged from something. Then he attached this to the cob house wall. Next he put the other end of the belt on a spool on which he'd also placed a spare belt, letting that belt momentarily hand loosely. He'd then impaled that spool on a long ten-penny nail on which the spool could freely rotate. Positioning the nail end far enough away to make that first belt taut, with a hammer he drove the nail into the cob house wall. By giving the crank a turn, his binder twine belt, or maybe a rubber band one, was empowered to turn that first spool. He was now ready to expand his operation!"

Mollie stopped to look at her audience. In her mind, she could see the side of that cob house as clearly as if that had occurred only yesterday. Now, for these kids to get the picture, it was difficult to explain. But she smiled and forged on, saying, "I hope I'm making sense in my describing this. For my brother, it was simple. By always using another nail-impaled spool for the other end of a belt, and remembering to slip the loop of a next belt on the spool before driving the nail in the wall, he ended up with a design of pulleys and tautly stretched belts.

"I can still see the smugly proud look on my brother's face as he turned that crank. That started the belt turning on the first spool which in turn propelled the connecting belts on a dozen or more other strategically placed spools."

Mollie had to chuckle. She said, "Of course, all that power didn't accomplish anything. But I'm sure it was good stimulation for my brother's active mind."

Then, in afterthought, she added, "Oh yes, those empty spools also made soap bubble blowers. Mom would let us get a little pan of water, and each of us could have a small sliver off a soap bar in our own little container, maybe a little sauce dish or a canning jar lid. By dipping one end of the spool into the water and sopping it up and down a few times on the soap, we made some suds. Then, with practiced deftness, we would get very good at covering the one end of the spool with a thin watery soapiness. By blowing ever so gently into the other end of the spool, a little bubble would form. And with practiced patience, we could nurse our little bubbles into humongous creations."

Caught up in the envisioning of those long ago scenes, Mollie's face was a pleasant reflection. She sort of laughed, adding, "At first, it was just for fun. We'd each be so proud and excited as a bubble gradually grew bigger and bigger. Then, carefully sliding a finger tightly over the hole at the blowing end of our spool, and giving the spool a quick jerk, the bubble would detach and float freely.

"But after awhile, invariably, competition would enter into that fun and Mom would have to take over as referee and disciplinarian."

Glancing at the two parents sitting there, listening to her, she said, "Basically, with kids, some things just don't ever change. When two kids play together, as a rule, things run smoothly. But add a third or fourth, and little quirks like jealousy, cattiness, maybe spitefulness, have a way of surfacing."

And Gail and Bruce knew exactly what she meant.

Twenty-three

Nebraska and Home Again

Bruce was already pressing the garage remote as he was turning into the driveway. Each watched as the big door rumbled up. They were back home again. There sat Gail's car, waiting, ready to get back again into the swing of things.

It was good to be home. And each of the four was busy with his own feelings about it.

Each knew this homecoming was different from any trip the family had returned from before. Bruce and Gail, adults as they were, couldn't put a finger on it specifically. Each was sensing having undergone some personal change. Even Holly and young Ethan seemed quieter, although neither of them was particularly delving into that.

They all shared in unloading the car and carrying the various stuff inside, taking it to wherever it belonged in the different rooms. But this was the first vacation trip ever that those Hinton family members were carrying in such a medley of feelings along with their luggage.

Typically, they used the bathrooms. And, routinely, Bruce and Gail looked over the house to determine that nothing had been disturbed during their absence. And, of course, they checked out the appliances to make sure that everything was still performing normally.

Holly phoned her best friend, Meredith, confirming her getting back. Strangely, and why, even she herself didn't understand, she declined her friend's urging her to run right over. Instead, she joined her dad and Ethan in the family room. They were relaxing comfortably there, and they could see Gail in the kitchen end of the big room, moving about, preparing food. After a moment, Holly joined her mother to help.

By now it had gotten to be past their regular evening dinnertime, and they had opted for just a grilled cheese sandwich with a dish of fruit.

It had been late noontime, about midway across Iowa, when they'd exited off I-80 at the famed Little Amana complex. They'd chosen the Olde Colony Haus restaurant with its reputation for Amish home cooking. And they'd sated themselves with the savory, very filling food that the Amish offer. Their meal had been served "family style," and this family had done some old fashioned "family-styled" eating!

Now, their stomachs were yet attesting to that late noontime strain, even in spite of all those many miles they'd since then ridden. Like coming on west through Des Moines, with still 150 miles or so to go, bringing them to the Missouri River and into Omaha, before finally making it on home.

Normally, the family would have eaten this snack-like meal at the breakfast bar, or even in front of the television set. But tonight, Gail was having Holly set the table in the dining area.

Noticeably, no doubt about it, that entire part of the big open room area had taken on a new and different feel. Even before they'd gone on their trip to Aunt Mollie's, Gail had begun to sense it. Now, while her hands were busy with preparing the sandwiches for getting them on the griddle, her mind was doing flip-flops, trying to analyze just what it was that was going on.

Earlier, on one of the trips from the car, she had stopped by the dining area table. Resting one corner of the toiletry case she was carrying on the edge of the table, she relaxed her other hand on the handle of her wheeled suitcase. She had just stood there, allowing herself to take in that scene, studying it.

Taking her luggage on into the bedroom, she was remembering about things Aunt Mollie had told them back in Illinois. And she was recalling things she'd had a chance to read about in some of those old journals on that second night there, upstairs in that old bedroom.

She was remembering especially of that incident with her standing within what was left of Ethan Bennett's circle of pine trees. Her own young Ethan had been there beside her.

She'd known that she would never ever forget her feelings that day. It had been strange, even awesome. But it had felt so pleasant. Being so quiet, breathing in deeply of that surrounding, she sensed a happy aliveness washing through her. She remembered the way young Ethan had squeezed her hand. He had smiled at her, making her know that he felt it too.

Also, as she had come back from her bedroom on her way back out to the car, with both hands empty, she'd paused again by the table. And again there was that atmosphere of sunshine. She was certain it was coming from those candlesticks. Nothing else in the room had been changed. Suddenly it was clear to her.

Standing there now, at the island counter, holding a slice of half-buttered bread in one hand, and the butter knife with a glob of butter in the other hand, she paused, smiling. She just knew she had the answer, and it was so wonderful.

That old wood from which those candlesticks were made was impregnated with Ethan Bennett's exuberant optimism. And, even now, that exuberance was dancing out from amidst that wood's luster, giving a cheeriness to the whole room. Aunt Mollie had said as much as she'd shared her own feelings of Whispering Pines.

Gail just stood there, her mind fairly churning. What a privilege it had been to spend those short days with Aunt Mollie and to be introduced to Whispering Pines and to so much of her family's old past. Now she was understanding the magnetism within that room.

Gail also understood that perhaps she was more open, more attuned, to acknowledging this presence of change within that area. All her life, with practice, on almost any given moment, she had become able to push out the stress of any day's sudden demand, allowing a soothing quietness to flow through her like a swig of tonic. As it purged, quietly and instantaneously, she'd become fortified, emotionally elevated. Every cell within her smiling and ready for life again!

So now, when the time was right, she would talk about all this with Bruce and the kids.

The family sat down at their usual places. There were the usual four plates, with each containing a very ordinary hot grilled cheese sandwich. And there were the four small dishes holding the typical fruits. Even the jaunty flowered tablecloth was one they used quite regularly. But tonight, everything felt special.

From the very first, with Gail's receiving that package from Aunt Mollie and her arranging those lovely old candlesticks on the table, the whole room had seemed to take on that new quality. It had taken on an air of importance. So even on those first few evenings, before they'd left on the trip to Illinois, they'd already noticed a certain niceness about the family dinners. Although no one had voiced it aloud, each had felt as if he was being treated to a special privilege, or something.

And now, tonight, with the family's having learned of all the history so intrinsically imbedded within the candlesticks, each in his own concept, was recognizing this air!

Each had learned of the many generations of heritage and could now better appreciate the richness reflecting from those heirlooms.

Sitting there now, watching the flickering candle flames rising from those three candlesticks, graduated in height as they were, that aura was unmistakable. Truly there was a quality of royalty, even a regalness, emitting from that lovely polished wood, a quality that somehow commanded respect. And, being within that radius, it was most comfortable.

Bruce felt good. So did Gail. Holly and Ethan felt the need to be quiet, trying to absorb this whole crazy thing.

Then, before they could take a bite, Bruce did a very astonishing thing, a thing so very out of character for him.

Out of his mouth came, "Wait a minute, guys," and as he said it, he was extending his hands, one out on either side, offering one to Holly and the other to Ethan.

With that, Gail, sitting at the foot of the table, followed Bruce's lead. Joining her hands with the kids, the four of them sat there, forming a little circle. This, definitely, was out of context, for sure.

Bruce went on, "I know this surprises you. It sure surprises me. But I feel like all of us are filled up with something different. Something that's new to us." Pausing a minute, looking at each of them, he went on, "Guys, it's hard to explain, but I have this sobering feeling that this ol' dad is just now coming of age!

"It looks like things are not going to be quite the same around this place. And, do you know what? I feel good about it! And, by Holy gees, I think we ought to talk to God about it!"

Just like that. And there was a deep quietness. In a heartbeat, each of the four had felt an extending out to each other. It was as if they were reaching a new level of closeness. It was all warm and nice. It felt pleasant. And not knowing what to expect next, each just bowed his head.

Again, Bruce hesitated. Then, he went on, "Dear God up there in heaven, uh…" and he hesitated again. Those pairs of hands in that little circle squeezed ever so slightly, waiting, a tender compassion passing through them.

Then he began again, "Dear Father, I feel a little crazy, uh…but, I like it! You know, we've just been exposed to a lot of stuff that we're not used to! We're going to have to have your help for all of us to get it all sorted and straightened out. But we do thank you for the privilege we've just had, making that trip out there to Illinois and getting to be with wise old Aunt Mollie. She has shown us how our little family is not sitting all alone here in Nebraska. We're actually a part of… well, she's made us see that we're connected with those rugged generations of the past. And she's also made us aware that the milestones we set…uh, I mean this little family sitting right here at this table…the milestones we set will affect and be connected with family descendants yet to come. Now…Holy Gees…God…that's pretty heavy stuff."

Bruce stopped. He took a big breath. Then, he went on. "Thank you, dear God, for showing us that we're a part of a bigger picture. We're gonna need your help and your guidance to make sure that our part of that bigger picture will be a worthy one. So, God...we're asking you to show us how. We're gonna need you to show us the way. Amen."

Again, Bruce glanced around at his little family. Gail seemed to be studying him. In the glimmer that flashed so briefly between them, she detected a different Bruce, a more matured Bruce...she could see it showing on his face. And also, in that same glimmer, she sensed that flicker of love passing between them that always warmed her while at the same time made goose bumps scurry up and down her body.

And this Bruce had just heard each one of his little family echo his own "Amen" as they loosened their hands, resting them in their laps.

Definitely, that little Hinton family in Hidden Hills, there in Bellevue, Nebraska, had just come through a very moving moment.

Suddenly Bruce's young son, the other man of the house, stood up. All the new feelings, the emotions, the mind circling, gathered up with him. And out of his mouth came a surprising statement of his own.

In a firm voice that displayed a self-confidence, to no one in particular, but very seriously, he said, "I am Ethan Hinton, and I've found out that I'm important. I've come from a long line of good family stock, and whatever I do is going to make a difference!"

Hearing that, Gail rolled her eyes. She let out a huge groan. She leaned back, throwing up both hands. "Oh...puh-leeze... somebody, send in the clowns!"

Then, looking at her daughter, "Holly, we have to live with these guys! Do you think we'll be able to stand the two of them?"

"We have to, Mom," Holly answered, smiling. "But we're going to have to be very careful. We don't want to injure their new masterfulness. We won't want to deflate them."

Everybody laughed. And they began to eat their cooling sandwiches.

But, deep down, down in the depths of each very being, each one of them was feeling thankful for the trip he'd just had. Each liked having learned the importance of discovering those connections with his past. Each knew this would forever be a very special highlight to remember throughout the rest of his future ahead.

No doubt, for as long as any member of this Bruce Hinton family would be the caretaker, there would be this very precious reminder reflecting from these three candlesticks made from Ethan Bennett's wood.

THE END

To My Readers:

Although my story, A Bridge of Wood, is fictitious, with fictional characters, a "factual" Harvey Bowen with his family did leave "some place" in Ohio during the latter half of the 1800s, settling on that Illinois acreage. Harvey did build the barn, with his family living in it until he finished the house.

His dreams, teamed up with his inventive mind had to be far advanced for those times, allowing him to produce that incredible place. Growing up, I was aware that Bowen descendants did exist in Danville, Illinois, although my family never met them.

Nearing the latter years of the 1800s, the Bowens, followed by a Philips family, had left the farm, and the Mortons, the couple who "raised" my mother, had moved there as tenant farmers, remaining for 24 years.

As life happened, my two oldest and my two youngest siblings were born in that house. Of the four of us in between, three were born in houses nearby, while I was born out-of-state during a venture my parents took on their own.

So, today, in 2002, with those long ago constant visits with our "acclaimed" grandparents, followed by my own family's actual living there from 1925 to 1930, my heart fairly dances with the wonderful reminiscing I am privileged to enjoy!

I spent my childhood in this "show place of the country" with the wind whooshing and whispering through that circle of pines!

Today, with my being aware that my 7 siblings with their memories are now dead, it is my hope that through these fictitionally written pages, our numerous Sollars family descendants can share in their own factual legacy of "Whispering Pines!"

NOTE: The original house that Mr. Bowen built burned down, probably during the 1940s, with another ordinary and typical farmhouse built to replace it. But, that will never affect my childhood memories from where they originated. Those remain intact!

About me...the author:

Whew...ee! 94 years old...unbelievable!!! But then, after all, I was born forever ago a couple of years before the ending of World War 1. I'm one of 8 siblings, with a large extended family, and I was born on the doorstep of fantastic change that's never quit.

While being terrifically busy with 3 kids, successful career, a 50-year marriage/love affair followed by a 13-year 2nd helping with both those wonderful guys up and dying on me, I've managed to experience some extensive traveling. Now, settled here in Plant City, Florida, I'm serious about writing... with another book nearly ready for querying a publisher.

But also, these days, I am detecting a competitive pull between my computer with its stack of blank pages and my big chair.

It seems, bottom line, continued bicycling and perseverance are in order to ensure the computer maintains the stronger pull!